THE BLACK ENTERPRISE

The Weight of Power

Nico Vaughn

Midnight Black Press

ISBN-13: 9781234567890
ISBN-10: 1477123456

Cover design by: Art Painter
Library of Congress Control Number: 2018675309
Printed in the United States of America

CONTENTS

Title Page

Copyright

1	1
2	33
3	51
4	74
5	98
6	125
7	145
8	161
9	199
10	216
11	235
12	249
13	262
14	275
15	288

16   297

17   316

18   337

19   346

20   363

1

S ome men demanded respect. Others were respected.

Ahmad Omari Miller, A.O. to the streets, never had to ask twice.

He stepped out of his Bentley, adjusting the cuffs of his tailored Tom Ford suit, and the valet was already moving. Not because A.O. said a word, but because he felt the weight of his presence.

The city lights bounced off his bust-down Rolex, diamonds flashing like a warning.

The Vegas night air carried the scent of money, sweat, and desperation, a smell only certain men could recognize.

A.O. knew it well.

It was the scent of men who needed something from him.

And A.O. didn't give out favors.

Inside the high-rise lounge, business was being handled. Not the kind with paper trails. The kind with bloodstains.

A.O. moved through the space like a king, six-three, built like a boxer, dark skin smooth, big beard neatly shaped, waves spinning under the dim lights. Every man in the room acknowledged him with a nod. Every woman noticed.

He wasn't loud with his power. He didn't have to be.

He made his way to the VIP section, his pace unbothered, unhurried. A nigga with real power never had to rush.

"Mr. Miller, your table is ready," a hostess purred, leading him to the corner booth, where Jah was already waiting.

Jahlil Pierson.

Blood brother. Same father, different mothers.

Nine years older, but somehow, A.O. had always been the one that felt like the big brother.

Jah had always been the book-smart one, college-educated, master's in finance, corporate suit-and-tie type. He had the stable family, the degrees, the life his mother had fought to give him.

A.O. had been raised differently. Their father, a Cubano gang leader who grew up in Brooklyn, had been around just enough to mold him. Teach him when to listen, when to move, when to make an example out of somebody.

Jah's mother had pushed their father away, kept Jah as far from the streets as possible. Private school. Suburbs. A world away from A.O.'s reality.

For a long time, Jah stayed clean. Built a family. Had a career as a hedge fund manager.

Until seven years ago.

When his oldest twins Josiah, & Cherish, died in a car accident on the way to prom.

That changed everything.

Jah and A.O. reconnected at the funeral. At first, it

was just brother shit. Grief. Time lost.

But A.O. saw something else, too.

Jah was moving millions in corporate money, the kind of clean money that could turn dirty cash into something real.

At the time, Jah needed extra money. He agreed to help, thinking it was just financial consulting. He didn't fully understand what that meant.

But soon, he was fully immersed in the game.

Jah wasn't moving weight or handling street shit. That was never his role. He made sure A.O.'s money was properly cleaned, put him on to real estate and investment plays, and even middle-manned major gang deals, ensuring new connects and opportunities were financially worthwhile.

But he was never comfortable.

And the deeper he got, the more he wanted to distance himself.

Still, the money was too good.

And A.O. wasn't letting him walk away.

Jah swirled his whiskey, watching the ice spin. His neatly lined mustache twitched as he smirked.

"Nigga, you later than your taxes."

A.O. barely smirked, settling into the leather seat across from him. "You know I don't rush for nobody."

Jah shook his head but didn't argue. That was the thing about A.O., his time was his own.

The conversation started easy. Money. Investments. Real estate moves. They weren't just running the streets anymore; they were owning them. Legitimately. Or at least close enough.

Jah was locked into the numbers, making sure the money stayed clean, the deals made sense, and the right plays were being made.

A.O. listened. Calculated. Every move had to go through him first.

And then, business turned to problems.

Specifically, Omar.

Jah leaned back, his brow furrowing slightly. "Your boy fucking up the money again." His tone was even, but sharp. "That nigga think the industry is the block."

A.O. exhaled slowly, rolling his diamond-studded Cartier wedding band between his fingers.

Jah wasn't wrong.

"Omar was supposed to be moving weight through the industry," Jah continued. "All these execs, managers, and artists he be around? He was supposed to have them buying. Instead, this nigga out here fronting them work like a fool. Now, we got missing product and no money coming back."

A.O. tapped his ring against the glass. Thinking. Calculating.

Omar had always been different. Not built for this. Too naive. Too trusting. Nigga really thought fame made him bulletproof.

A.O. saw it every time they met up. Omar, walking into rooms with that easy, laid-back energy, locs hanging past his shoulders, dressed in sweats and slides like he was just another regular nigga instead of a multi-platinum rapper. No security. No jewelry.

No sense.

A.O. had tried to put him on game, but Omar still thought because he rapped about the streets, he understood them.

He didn't.

And it was about to cost him.

Jah shook his head and took another sip of his drink. "I don't give a fuck how many plaques he got. If he ain't bringing money back, then he's a liability. Nigga think because he famous, nobody gon' press him."

A.O. said nothing, just watched the way the light hit the glass in his hand. Jah wasn't wrong. The money wasn't adding up, and A.O. wasn't the type to let a nigga play with his bottom line.

Jah sighed and sat forward. "You got too many niggas depending on you to be covering his mistakes forever. Either he makes shit right, or you make sure it ain't your problem anymore."

A.O. exhaled slowly, set his glass down, and met Jah's eyes.

"I'll handle it."

Jah studied him for a second, then nodded. That was the thing about A.O., when he said he'd handle something, he meant it.

And when A.O. handled something, niggas didn't get second chances.

The drive home was quiet. Not the kind of silence that came with peace, but the kind that weighed heavy. The kind that meant something was on his mind.

A.O. gripped the steering wheel with one hand, his other resting against his chin as he stared at the road ahead. The Vegas skyline blurred past him, neon lights glowing against the black night, but he barely saw it. His mind was somewhere else.

Money was never the issue. He had money.

More than enough to live any life he wanted. More than enough to give his wife everything she'd ever asked for. More than enough to ensure that his daughter would never know struggle, never want for anything.

And yet, he couldn't shake the feeling that it could all be taken away.

Not by another nigga. Not by some reckless move in the streets.

By something bigger.

A raid. A federal investigation. A fucking RICO case.

No matter how smart he moved, how many cops were on his payroll, how deep his ties ran, there was always a risk. Always.

A.O. had built something bigger than just a drug empire. This wasn't small-time. He had properties, businesses, money washing through half the city. The gang, his gang, had grown beyond street corners. This was an operation. A machine.

And machines didn't stop overnight.

Unless somebody tore them down.

Unless a nigga made the wrong move.

Unless he made the wrong move.

The thought sat heavy in his chest, a feeling he had learned to ignore over the years but could never really shake. It was worse now. Now that he had Calia and Malia.

His wife stirred beside him, shifting in her seat.

Calia's long legs were crossed at the ankle, toned and glowing against the soft leather. Her chestnut hair caught the moonlight in waves, cascading over her shoulder. Even in something simple, leggings, heels, and an oversized hoodie, she looked like money. Glossed lips pursed, lashes low, but her whole body buzzed with tension.

She could feel it.

She always could.

She didn't say anything right away, just watched him, those big brown eyes flickering under the passing streetlights. She knew him too well to ask him what was wrong. If she asked, he'd just tell her it was nothing.

And she'd know he was lying.

The house was quiet when they stepped inside. Their daughter was already asleep, the soft hum of the baby monitor filling the living room as Calia set down her purse.

A.O. pulled off his suit jacket, rolling his shoulders before dropping it onto the couch. He loosened his collar next, undoing the top two buttons of his shirt, but the tension didn't leave his body.

Calia didn't press him. Not yet.

She walked to the kitchen, grabbed two glasses, and poured them both a drink.

When she handed him the glass, he finally looked at her.

Calia.

His wife. His everything.

She had been there since the beginning, since he was a broke-ass teenager selling dime bags outside the corner store.

She had been fourteen when she walked into his life, all attitude and ambition, talking shit to him in their high school hallways. Not judging him when she found out he was hustling.

Back then, the weight was small. Bags in his pockets,

a few hundred dollars a day if he was lucky. He had nothing to his name except a dream and the hustle to make it happen.

And she had believed in him before anybody else did.

Calia had always been a hustler herself. That's what he loved about her. She had never been the type to sit back and wait for shit to happen. She made it happen.

When they graduated high school, she didn't want to do college. She wanted to make her own money, but she hated working under niggas who didn't respect her.

The first time she stepped into a strip club, she had been seventeen, sneaking in with a fake ID just to get a feel for the place.

By eighteen, she was onstage.

She had hated it at first. Hated the way the owner ran shit, hated how he took advantage of the girls, how the money was good but never quite enough.

And A.O. had watched her go from hating it to running it.

She learned the game fast, became the top earner,

started pulling strings behind the scenes. She had a plan to get out.

And then A.O. made his first real move.

By the time he was twenty-one, he had stacked enough to buy the club outright.

She had been right there when he signed the paperwork, when he handed that triflin' old owner a buyout and took over the spot that had once owned her.

It wasn't just about the money. It was about power.

The club became the foundation, a front, a hub, a business that made them both rich in different ways.

Calia had used it to build her brand.

A.O. had used it to move weight.

It wasn't long before they were too deep to turn back.

At first, Calia hadn't minded. She was on her own grind, trying to make something out of nothing.

YouTube had started as a side hustle, makeup tutorials between shifts, vlogs that barely got views.

Then one video blew up.

And another.

And another.

By the time A.O. proposed, she had told him, "I'm done. I ain't stripping no more."

And he had promised her she wouldn't have to.

She had begged him to go legit with her. Take the money they had and build something real.

He had told her he would think about it.

But he never did.

She had gone all-in on her dream, and it paid off. World-famous YouTuber. Brand deals, sponsorships, investments in luxury real estate.

A.O. had built his own legit empire too.

But he had never let go of the streets.

And now, it was getting harder and harder to keep the two worlds separate.

Calia leaned against the counter, watching him over the rim of her glass. She was studying him, waiting for him to speak.

"You tired?" she finally asked.

A.O. took a slow sip of his drink. He was exhausted. But he just shook his head.

She set her glass down.

"You wanna tell me what's on your mind?"

A.O. stayed quiet for a second, then shrugged. "Shit you already know."

Calia exhaled, rubbing her fingers against her temple.

He already knew what she was gonna say.

We can leave this shit behind.

We got more money than we'll ever need.

We got Mahlia to think about.

And she was right.

She was always right.

But he also knew what she didn't.

It wasn't that simple.

Not anymore.

He had built too much. Expanded too far. He wasn't just some nigga selling on the block anymore.

This was bigger than him.

Bigger than them.

And if he stepped away now? If he tried to go legit?

Somebody else would take it.

Somebody worse.

Somebody who didn't have a code.

Calia walked over, slipping her arms around his

waist. She rested her head against his chest, and A.O. finally let out a slow breath, pressing a kiss to the top of her head.

"I just want you safe," she murmured.

"I am," he said, but they both knew that wasn't true.

Not really.

Not as long as he was still in the game.

And Calia knew it too well.

Which was why she never stopped waiting for the day he would finally say, "I'm done."

◆ ◆ ◆

The house was warm, filled with the quiet hum of the baby monitor and soft R&B playing in the background.

Nya slipped off her sneakers by the door, stretching out her sore legs from another fourteen-hour shift at the hospital. Exhaustion settled deep in her bones, but she still smiled.

Because unlike most nights, she wasn't coming

home to an empty house or a quiet studio.

Omar was already upstairs, sitting on the floor of the nursery, Alya resting on his chest.

His locs were loose, a few strands falling into his face as he rubbed soft circles on their daughter's back, his head leaned against the rocking chair. His eyes were closed, but Nya knew he wasn't asleep.

She leaned against the doorway, arms crossed. "Why didn't you put her in her crib?"

Omar smirked, eyes still shut. "She wanted to sleep on me. You know I can't say no."

Nya chuckled, stepping inside. She'd be lying if she said it didn't make her heart swell every time she saw them like this.

Because whatever flaws Omar had, whatever frustrations lingered between them, he was an amazing father.

Patient. Present. Loving.

The kind of father Nya wished she'd had.

Her own father had never been there, not emotionally. He had spent all his energy trying to mold her into the opposite of her sister.

Calia had been the rebel. The wild one. The disappointment.

So Nya had been their project. The perfect daughter. The good one.

She had loved dance since she was a child, moving effortlessly, feeling alive in a way nothing else made her feel. From high school dance team to majorette at college, it had been her world.

But none of that had mattered.

Because once, when she was seven, she had said, "I want to be a doctor when I grow up."

And her parents had never let her forget it.

They pushed her. Hard. Not because they saw her passion, but because they wanted her to be better than Calia.

So, she did what they wanted.

She studied harder than anyone. Graduated top of her class. Got into medical school. Became a cosmetic surgeon.

And she was good at it.

But it was never what she wanted.

That dream, the real one, had never died.

Now, she had her eye on a dance studio for sale. A space where she could build something real for herself. A place with a two-bedroom luxury condo above it.

It was perfect.

But she hadn't told Omar yet.

Because she already knew what he would think.

That it wasn't enough.

That a two-bedroom condo wouldn't fit the family he wanted to keep growing.

He wanted more kids. He had already started bringing it up, casually slipping comments about giving Alya a sibling, about Nya staying home and letting him take care of everything.

If she told him about the studio, about how perfect

she thought it was, how she already saw herself living and breathing in that space, he'd only see how small it was.

How it wasn't made for the life he wanted for them.

And he loved her. She knew that. But love didn't erase the past.

Omar had changed. He wasn't the same man she had met all those years ago, back when he was a broke underground rapper barely getting by.

But sometimes, it still felt like he was trying to prove himself.

Prove that he could take care of her.
Prove that he wasn't that struggling college kid anymore.
Prove that he had earned her trust after breaking it once before.

Because there had been other women.

Not anymore. Not since they got married, not since Alya was born.

But back when he was still new to money, new to fame, new to the attention, there had been moments. Mistakes.

And even though he had done everything right since then, even though he had given her no reason to doubt him...

Somewhere deep down, she still did.

Because the late nights at the studio, the hush phone calls, the times he left suddenly in the middle of the night, they reminded her of the past.

She didn't tell him that, though.

O thought she just didn't trust him to take care of their family.

And maybe a part of him was right.

Because while she had been scraping through college, barely sleeping, drowning in loans, he had been a broke rapper hustling just to be heard.

By the time he finally got signed, she was in her residency, exhausted, barely keeping their relationship together.

And back then? She hadn't trusted that he would ever make it.

Not because he wasn't talented, Omar had always been talented. But because talent didn't pay the bills.

But then he did make it.

And she had to watch him live out his wildest dreams while she spent her days in surgery, drowning in exhaustion.

And he had enjoyed it. The women, the attention, the lifestyle.

Until he didn't.

Until it had cost him almost everything.

Now, Omar was different.

The chains, the designer fits, the fast cars, he had let all that go. Now, he was all sweats, tees. Riding his bike around the city unless he had Alya with him.

But Nya still felt like she was waiting for the other shoe to drop.

Waiting for him to get bored of this new life.
Waiting for the past to repeat itself.
Waiting for him to slip up.

And what scared her the most?

If he wasn't cheating… then what was he hiding?

Because Omar wasn't the type to move sloppy.

If he was sneaking around, if he was leaving in the middle of the night, if he was taking hush phone calls when he thought she wasn't looking.

Then whatever he was involved in was bigger than just another woman.

And that was even more dangerous.

Omar reached for her hand, lacing his fingers through hers. "Nya, I got you. You know that, right?"

She swallowed, nodding. "I know."

But she also knew that promises were just words until they weren't.

Omar studied her for a long moment, then smirked, his voice dropping lower. "You know what else?"

"What?"

He leaned in, lips grazing her ear. "I think you should quit your job and give me another baby."

Nya's eyes snapped up, but Omar just grinned, full of mischief, full of love.

She scoffed, pushing at his chest. "Boy, shut up."

"What? You scared?"

"Of what?"

He kissed her, slow and deep, making her breath catch. "Of how bad you want it."

Nya rolled her eyes, but her pulse was racing. She pushed off him, standing up. "I need a shower."

Omar smirked, watching her walk away. "Want some company?"

She glanced back at him, teasing. "Mmm... Maybe next time."

Omar chuckled, shaking his head as she disappeared down the hall.

Yeah. He'd get her to quit eventually.

He just had to wear her down first.

◆ ◆ ◆

The morning sun poured through the massive windows, bathing the kitchen in warm light. The scent of fresh coffee, eggs, and cinnamon toast filled the air, blending with the soft hum of R&B playing from the built-in speakers.

At the stove, Geneva moved with effortless precision, flipping eggs in one pan while stirring oatmeal in another, all while keeping an eye on the kids. Dressed in a fitted neutral-toned lounge set, her sleek bob effortlessly laid, she carried herself like a woman who had it all under control.

Jah stood at the island, dressed in a tailored navy suit, his Rolex catching the morning light as he scrolled through emails while sipping coffee.

"I already packed the triplets' bags," he said smoothly.

Geneva barely looked up as she plated food. "Did you put extra snacks for Trinity? You know she eats more than the other two."

Jah smirked, setting his phone down. "Already handled. You know I got it."

She nodded, sliding a plate in front of him before turning to the kids.

Across the island, Chasiti sat with her phone in hand, scrolling lazily as her big, thick curls framed her face. She wore sweatpants and an oversized hoodie, her usual relaxed but effortless style. At fourteen, she was already taller than Geneva, her personality a perfect mix of sharp wit and quiet intensity.

"You're not eating?" Geneva arched a brow.

"I'm fasting."

Geneva sighed. "For what?"

Chasiti shrugged. "Discipline."

Jah chuckled, shaking his head. "Girl, if you don't eat this damn pancake." He slid the plate toward her.

Chasiti rolled her eyes but picked up a fork, taking a slow, dramatic bite just to avoid an argument.

The triplets, Trinity, Serenity, and J, or Justin when he was acting up, sat in their booster seats, giggling as they played with their food. Serenity was the loudest, always trying to keep up with her older siblings. Trinity, true to her name, was the most centered, quiet but observant. J, the only boy, was already a little ladies' man, flashing dimples at Geneva when she cut his pancakes into smaller bites.

Ashanti, ten years old and full of energy, danced in her seat, singing along to the music playing in the background. She had a big, toothy smile and danced in her chair like the music was made just for her.

Jah reached for his coffee just as his phone buzzed on the counter.

UNKNOWN NUMBER.

He flipped it over, ignoring it.

Seconds later, a text preview flashed across the screen.

"Time's up, J. Call me before I call you."

His grip tightened around his mug. His face didn't change, but the weight of everything pressed down on his chest like a slow-moving avalanche.

The gambling had started after the twins died.

At first, it was just a distraction. Something to fill the spaces where grief seeped in. A way to quiet the guilt, to silence the constant replay of what-ifs in his mind.

Then, it became a fix.

Vegas was the worst place to lose control. He could go to the gas station and see a slot machine. The casinos were always waiting, whispering promises of a way out. And when that wasn't enough, he had found the back rooms, the private tables, the underground games where real money moved.

For a while, it hadn't been a problem.

Then it had become the only problem.

When he reconnected with A.O. at the twins' funeral, it had been perfect timing.

A.O. had money. Legit investments, real estate, business opportunities, and Jah was the man who could make that money move.

His little brother was already deep in the streets,

but he wanted to be bigger. He wanted his empire structured, protected, cleaned.

And Jah?

He could do that.

The extra money A.O. paid him made it easy at first. A cushion. He justified the gambling because it wasn't coming out of their household funds.

But that just made it worse.

Because eventually, the extra money wasn't enough.

He started dipping into his own accounts. Then their savings. Then, when the losses kept piling up, he started taking from work.

It had been small at first. Numbers that wouldn't raise alarms. Just enough to cover a bad night.

Then, just enough to cover two.

And then, before he knew it, he was in deep.

The hole was too big. The dirt was piling in faster than he could climb out.

And the worst part?

It wasn't even his money anymore.

"You okay?"

Geneva's voice pulled him back.

He blinked, snapping back to reality. "Yeah," he said smoothly, forcing a smile. "We gotta get going."

Chasiti rolled her eyes, but she got up, sliding her phone into her hoodie pocket. Ashanti grabbed her backpack, still humming to herself. The triplets squealed as Jah kissed Geneva's cheek, heading toward the door.

Geneva wiped her hands on a dish towel, glancing toward the counter.

There was a bill sitting there, unopened.

Her lips pressed together.

Jah always handled things like that.

Still, she picked it up, just for a second, before setting it right back down.

She had no reason to be worried.

None at all.

2

The bass thumped low through the walls, vibrating through the glass windows that overlooked the city skyline. The studio, a sleek, state-of-the-art space housed within Black Dominion Enterprises, was more than just a place to record.

It was a fortress.

On the surface, it was one of the most exclusive recording studios in Vegas, reserved for top-tier artists under Omar's label. A whole network of soundproofed booths, production rooms, and a boardroom used for executive meetings and label negotiations. But beneath the surface, it was part of the business, the same way the attached modeling agency was.

The models were dual-purpose. Some were

legitimate, signed to campaigns, booked for videos, moving like professionals. Others? They had secondary roles, acting as distractions, couriers, or sometimes just another way to clean money.

And Jaylen? He had an office here too.

He wasn't there for business. He was there for Omar.

A babysitting job, courtesy of A.O.

Jaylen hated it. Hated him.

But orders were orders.

He didn't even have to have cameras in the room to see who was watching Omar too hard. He had eyes everywhere.

But Omar?

He wasn't paying attention.

He was in his zone, locked into the music, sitting in the plush leather chair at the console. His fingers tapped idly against the table as he listened back to the beat, 808s knocking, layered over the sample he flipped last night.

It was clean. Almost perfect.

"You hear that?" he asked, tapping the engineer's arm. "Turn my reverb down a little. It's bleeding into the adlibs."

The engineer nodded, adjusting the mix. Omar barely noticed the lingering tension in the air.

Then, a soft voice cut through the music.

"Damn, you really a genius with this shit."

Omar smirked before even looking up. He already knew who it was.

Sienna.

She was signed to Black Dominion Modeling. Booked for videos, exclusive events. But lately? She had been spending more time in his studio than in front of a camera.

Omar knew why.

She was checking for him. Had been for a minute.

She had that look, light brown skin, long wavy

weave, full lips glossed up just enough, always in something tight. She knew how to play the role, knew how to be seen.

Omar wasn't oblivious. He just wasn't entertaining it.

At least, that's what he told himself.

He glanced up from the screen, flashing that easy, unreadable grin. "I told you, this what I do."

Sienna smiled, stepping closer, her Chanel perfume cutting through the scent of smoke and cognac.

"You let everybody see you work like this?" she asked, tilting her head.

Omar chuckled, taking a sip of his drink. "Only the people I trust."

Her eyes lit up at that, and he knew he had her. Not that it mattered.

This wasn't anything serious.

Just a distraction.

And that was the problem.

Because while Omar was distracted, something in the room shifted.

A presence.

Subtle, but off.

Omar felt it before he saw it.

The way the air changed, the way the energy in the space pulled in a different direction.

He glanced up, scanning the room, and then.

His eyes landed on him.

Some random nigga, standing against the back wall, watching him too hard.

Omar frowned slightly.

"Who the fuck is that?" He thought.

He kept his posture relaxed, but his mind was already moving. He made it a point to know who was in his space. Industry heads, artists, execs, niggas who needed to be here.

And this nigga?

Omar didn't know him.

& he didn't like that.

His jaw tightened slightly, but he kept his tone light as he leaned toward Abdul, his main producer.

"Aye," he muttered low. "Who he with?"

Abdul glanced up, following Omar's gaze. His face shifted slightly.

"He came with Mecca."

Omar exhaled slow.

Mecca was one of his artists, but he had a bad habit of bringing the wrong niggas around. Too friendly. Too trusting.

Omar let his gaze linger on the unfamiliar dude.

Then, like clockwork, the nigga made his move.

He pushed off the wall, straightening his jacket before making his way toward Omar's section.

Sienna leaned in again, her lips just inches from Omar's ear. "You tryna leave soon? I was thinking maybe—"

"Hold that thought," Omar murmured, his focus shifting fully as the stranger pulled up.

The nigga grinned, too familiar, too comfortable.

"Ayo, big homie, I just wanna say, I been rocking with your shit for a minute. That last tape? Crazy. You really putting on for the city."

Omar smirked, nodding once. "Good looks."

But he wasn't smiling anymore.

This wasn't admiration.

This was a setup.

The nigga wasn't walking away.

He was planting himself in the circle.

Before Omar could say anything, the studio door swung open.

Jaylen stepped in the room like he owned the shit.

6'5, broad as hell, high-yellow damn near glowing under the dim lights. His curly taper fade was fresh, his dark eyes already sweeping the room.

Omar barely acknowledged him, but Jaylen clocked the unfamiliar dude immediately.

And he didn't hesitate.

"Who the fuck is this?"

The studio went silent.

The stranger barely had time to react before Jaylen was on him.

The dude stammered, grinning like he could laugh it off. "Ayo, chill, man. I'm Mecca's cousin—"

Jaylen cut his eyes toward Mecca, who had the good sense to look nervous.

"Mecca." Jaylen's voice was calm. Too calm. "Why the fuck you always bringing niggas nobody know?"

Mecca shifted. "It ain't like that, bro. He cool—"

Jaylen wasn't trying to hear it.

He turned back to the dude, stepping even closer. "You been in here all night, watching niggas. Ain't said a word 'til now. What the fuck you on?"

Omar moved then, pushing off his chair.

"Jay—"

Jaylen didn't even glance at him.

"You vouching for him, O?"

Omar hesitated.

And that said everything.

Jaylen's lip curled. "That's what I thought."

Then, without a word, he reached forward and snatched the chain off the dude's neck.

The entire room tensed.

Jaylen dangled it, shaking his head. "Coming through this bitch rocking a fake ass chain, trying to fit in. Nigga, you don't belong here."

The dude stepped back immediately. "Ayo, chill, bro. It ain't even like that—"

Jaylen didn't move.

"Get the fuck out."

No arguments.

No second chances.

The dude turned and damn near ran out.

Mecca didn't say shit.

Omar sighed, rubbing his forehead. "Nigga, you always gotta be extra?"

Jaylen tossed the chain onto the table. "Nah. Y'all niggas always too relaxed."

Jaylen's phone buzzed. He pulled it out, checked the screen, and his mood shifted.

He shoved his phone toward Omar. "Read that."

Omar frowned. The text hit like a bullet.

"That nigga you just pressed? One of the jack boys from Rome's crew."

Omar's stomach tightened.

Jack boys.

Niggas who set people up. Who caught you slipping, lined you up, made you think it was all love before they made a move.

And this one had been in his studio. Watching. Waiting.

Jaylen leaned back in his seat, voice even. "That's why I be on ten."

Omar exhaled slow, gripping his glass.

Jaylen didn't say anything else. He didn't need to.

Omar knew what the fuck it meant.

Niggas was watching.

And they thought he was an easy lick.

The waiter reappeared, moving silently as he set down a bottle of Rémy Martin Louis XIII, refilling their glasses. The private room was high up, overlooking the Vegas skyline, the neon lights casting a subtle glow against the sleek black walls.

A.O. barely noticed. His focus was on Jah.

His brother had spent years perfecting the art of control. Jah never showed his cards, not in the boardroom, not in the streets, not even at home. But tonight? Something was different.

Jah took a slow sip of his drink before setting it down carefully, his fingers tapping against the glass. It was a nervous tick. One A.O. had only seen a handful of times.

A.O. exhaled slowly, his fingers tightening around his own glass. This wasn't supposed to be Jah's life.

Jah had already made it out. Had done what A.O. never could, went to college, built a career, started a family. He wasn't supposed to be here.

And yet, here they were.

Because of him.

A.O. had pulled him back into this world. Had given him a seat at the table, knowing damn well Jah was never meant to sit here.

And maybe that had been selfish.

But when they reconnected seven years ago, A.O. hadn't been thinking about consequences. He had only been thinking about how useful Jah could be.

A hedge fund manager? A nigga who understood money, real estate, investments?

He needed that.

And Jah needed money.

It had made sense at the time.

But now?

Now A.O. wasn't so sure.

Jah didn't belong in this world, not the way he did.

And A.O. wasn't sure if he regretted pulling him in, or if he regretted the fact that Jah was still here.

A.O. tapped the edge of his glass, watching him carefully. "You sure you good?"

Jah chuckled under his breath, shaking his head. "Nigga, I said I'm good."

A.O. leaned back, rubbing his chin. He could press him, call him out right now, put the pressure on him, but Jah wasn't the type to fold easy.

Instead, he played it smooth. "Alright then. If you good, let's move on."

Jah nodded, relaxing slightly, like he had just passed a test.

A.O. pulled out his phone, swiping through the mock-ups for the new high-end lounge.

The location was prime, just off the Strip, sleek design, built for the elite. No random tourists, no bullshit. This was the type of place that catered to the city's biggest spenders.

He turned the screen toward Jah. "We securing the land next month. I want everything locked in before we start building."

Jah studied the images, nodding. "It's clean."

"That's the point. No bullshit, no extras. Members only. This ain't for just anybody."

Jah exhaled through his nose, rolling his glass between his fingers. "4.5 million is a big move."

A.O. smirked. "That 4.5 million will make bigger moves."

Jah let out a short laugh, but it didn't quite reach his eyes. "You really don't stress about shit, huh?"

A.O. arched a brow. "What's to stress about?"

Jah didn't answer.

Because he couldn't.

His little brother was sitting here talking about dropping nearly five million like it was nothing, while Jah was drowning.

No, suffocating.

In bets he thought he could flip.

In debts he couldn't climb out of.

In the weight of knowing the one nigga who could fix this, who could wipe his slate clean in a second, was sitting right across from him.

And he couldn't ask.

Wouldn't.

Because it was already bad enough that A.O. was his boss.

Bad enough that he had to take money from his little brother to maintain the life he built.

He couldn't let him be his savior too.

Jah took a slow sip of his drink. He had to stall.

"I'm not saying it's a bad move," he started, keeping his tone light. "I just think... why now?"

A.O. frowned slightly. "Why not?"

Jah shrugged, setting his glass down. "We still flipping the last spot. Maybe we should push this back a few months. Just... let things settle."

A.O. studied him, his gaze sharp. "You not feeling

this play?"

Jah shook his head. "It's not that."

"Then what?"

Jah was thinking fast now.

Because he couldn't say the truth.

He couldn't say, The pipeline's jammed.

He couldn't say, Every shell company I touch is under review.

He couldn't say, I moved too much, too fast, trying to fix my own mess — and now the money's glowing red.

So instead, he leaned into caution.

"I just think we should be smart about how we move it," he said smoothly. "Let's not rush it."
A.O. exhaled, leaning back.

Jah had never questioned his moves like this before.

And that didn't sit right.

But A.O. wasn't about to press it.

Not tonight.

He nodded slowly, picking up his drink. "Aight. We'll talk."

Jah felt himself relax, just slightly.

A.O. clocked that too.

Yeah.

Something was definitely off.

And A.O. was gonna find out what.

3

The bassline rumbled low, shaking the walls of the private studio suite. Expensive speakers hummed with an unreleased track, thick with layered vocals and crisp percussion. The air was laced with weed smoke, cologne, and the sharp burn of premium tequila.

Omar leaned back into the black leather couch, one ankle resting on his knee, scrolling through his phone while half-listening to the producer tweak the mix. His inbox was flooded, artists locking in beats, managers setting up sessions, execs asking for favors. It was a never-ending cycle of money, music, and motion.

This was why the gang kept him around.

He wasn't the best at street work. He wasn't cut out for running corners or handling enforcement. But what he did bring? No one else in A.O.'s crew could.

He had access.

Omar wasn't just *in* the industry, he was moving weight through it. The kind of product that never touched the streets, never needed to be passed off in alleys or trap houses. His clients weren't fiends or low-level pushers. They were executives, artists, producers, label heads. The ones with money, power, and the protection of fame.

And that made him more valuable than any shooter.

Across the room, a conversation was happening that he already knew was about to land at his feet.

A label exec, one of the biggest in the business, sat on a stool near the booth, laughing, talking shit with a couple of his artists. He was old money, the type that didn't move sloppy, the type that didn't need to flex because his power was felt in every room he stepped into.

Omar let the moment stretch, waiting. He already knew what was coming.

And sure enough, a few minutes later, the exec's gaze drifted over, locking onto him.

Omar smirked, rolling his shoulders before sitting up.

The exec chuckled, shaking his head. "Nigga, you already know."

Omar laughed under his breath, setting his phone down. Yeah. He knew.

This wasn't about beats, tracks, or features.

This was about product.

"Give us a minute," Omar said, motioning the others out.

The exec took a slow sip of his drink. "Start with three. We'll re-up before the weekend."

Omar kept his tone casual, slipping his hands into his pockets. "I'll set it up."

The exec clapped him on the shoulder. "I'ma send my guy your way."

Omar smirked, already typing the drop-off details into his phone. "Bet."

The morning light poured through the floor-to-ceiling windows of Jah's luxury office, bouncing off the glass walls and polished oak desk. The space was immaculate, designed to reflect power, control, success.

But Jah?

He felt none of that right now.

His leg bounced under the desk, fingers drumming lightly against the polished wood. His watch felt heavier than usual, his tailored suit a little tighter.

His phone lit up for the third time in ten minutes.

UNKNOWN CALLER.

But he knew who the fuck it was.

A slow, burning tension coiled in his chest. He had been avoiding this call all morning, knowing exactly how it would go.

He exhaled through his nose, pressed his lips together, then, with a forced sense of calm, he picked up.

"Yeah."

The voice on the other end was smooth. Too smooth.

"Jah, my boy. Thought maybe you forgot about me."

Jah leaned back in his chair, keeping his tone even. "Nah, I don't forget shit. Just been busy."

A short laugh. "Busy, huh? Busy making money, I hope."

Jah's grip tightened around the phone.

"I told you. I got you."

A pause. Then, "See, that's the thing. You keep saying that. But I ain't seen nothing hit my account yet."

$100K. That's what he owed. The number was a weight, pressing against his chest, tightening inch by inch.

He could have easily fixed this, A.O. had it. Hell, he had ten times that in liquid cash.

But he wasn't about to ask his little brother for help.

"You'll get it," Jah said, keeping his voice smooth, unbothered. "Give me a little more time."

Another laugh. "Jah, Jah, Jah. You a numbers guy, right? A hedge fund nigga. You know how interest works."

Jah didn't respond.

"Time ain't free, my boy."

Jah could hear the shift in tone. Less friendly. Less patient.

He tapped the desk again.

"Stay calm. Stay in control."

"I know that."

"Good. Then you know next time I call, I ain't gonna be as friendly."

The line went dead.

Jah let the phone drop onto the desk, exhaling slowly.

The walls felt like they were closing in.

His perfect life, his wife, his kids, his career, his reputation, it was all sitting on a foundation made of sand.

One wrong move, and it could all come crashing down.

And nobody knew.

Not his wife. Not A.O. Not a single soul.

Jah rubbed his hands down his face, exhaling through his nose.

He had to fix this.

And he had to do it before it was too late.

The low hum of clippers buzzed against A.O.'s fade, the scent of aftershave and burning incense mixing with the faint aroma of cash being counted. The shop was closed to the public, the only people inside were his crew, called in by A.O. for a check-in.

This was about business. Money.

A.O. didn't touch street money.

They brought it to him coded, counted, already converted.

H ran it through a network of trusts, shell companies, and offshore accounts, then sent it back polished. Legal. Untraceable.

A.O. leaned back in the chair, letting the barber work, but his attention was on his men in the room with him, The Circle. The founding fathers of The Black Enterprise.

Jaylen was the first to speak, setting down a matte black USB on the counter. "Casino's cleared. All debts collected. Transfers split between the three shells. You'll see it by noon."

Jaylen Cooper. A.O.'s most loyal soldier. The underground casino runner, the man who collected debts and payments from the businesses TBE protected. If a nigga owed money, Jaylen got it. If someone refused to pay, Jaylen made them. Trigger-happy, with a nickname Switch, that he hated so much you better now let him hear you say it or you'd find out exactly how he got it. Ruthless. Not to be fucked with.

And loyal to the death.

A.O. gave him a slow nod, trusting that the count was right. Jaylen didn't play about money.

Next, Brandon stepped up, unlocking his phone and sliding it across the counter. The screen showed a masked dashboard, several deposits confirmed, corners all labeled by street code.

Brandon. The quiet one. Calculated, always moving in silence. He was the one who pushed other gangs out of their spots, set up new corners, and made sure TBE's presence was felt. Where Jaylen handled the big-money collections, Brandon controlled the streets.

If you were in TBE territory, you paid for the privilege.

A.O. exhaled, satisfied. The money was moving, and everything was running smooth.

Dru Harp. NBA name. TBE muscle.

The baller in the league who was most likely to knock a nigga out on the court.

A.O. brought him in back when he was just a broke teenager with a scholarship and pressure at home. Fronted him a package to get off on the campus elites. Once he cleared that he never looked back, he was making

Now? He had money. Fame. 35-million-dollar contract. But no amount of money could ever repay A.O.

So he still moved product in private suites with team owners and afterparties with coaches who ran through crack like he ran through niggas on the court.

He didn't need the crew. He stayed because he liked breaking jaws.

When shit got loud, he sent Dru as a warning.

A.O. gave him a small nod.

Deonte stepped forward with a cold smirk, sliding a manila folder across the counter instead of tech. Paper. Old school.

He was old head. Ran with A.O. and Jah's pops back in the day. When their father got locked up, Deonte thought he was next in line. But that didn't happen.

A.O. took over. By the time their father was killed in prison, A.O. had transformed The Black Enterprise into something Deonte never could.

A.O. had cleaned house, got rid of the old heads, brought in fresh faces.

Except for Deonte.

A.O. kept him around, but he peeped the jealousy.

"Collections from our side. But we got some new niggas trying to step on toes." His tone was casual, but there was always a little extra weight when he talked to A.O. "I can handle that, though. Unless you got another plan?"

A.O. met his gaze, unreadable. "We'll talk," he said simply.

Deonte nodded once, leaning back, satisfied. For now.

Then Omar stepped up. And the moment he did, A.O. already knew something was off.

Omar cleared his throat, shifting his weight. He wasn't stupid, he knew everybody was watching. "Aye... so, my runner got hit."

Silence.

Jah sighed, pinching the bridge of his nose. "Nigga, just say you fucked up."

Omar's jaw clenched. "It wasn't that, bro. Niggas was waiting on him."

A.O. cut the barber a look. The man nodded, pulling the cape off and stepping back.

Not a muscle in A.O.'s face moved, on the inside, he was tight.

A runner? Still?

That was the problem with Omar. Still moving like this was a corner hustle instead of a multi-million-dollar operation. The rest of them had evolved. Jaylen washed casino money through event venues and charity raffles. Brandon cycled corner taxes through real estate LLCs and fake logistics contracts. Dru funneled his dice game cuts into a chain of luxury car rentals his girl fronted on paper.

The cash never touched daylight. By the time it reached Jah, it was already dressed in a suit and tie, walking into investment accounts with tax returns and W-2s to match.

Omar? Still sending some twenty-year-old through the city with a duffel bag like this was 2003.

That's what made it hot.

Now, all eyes were on Omar.

A.O. stood up slow, adjusting his watch. "How much?"

Omar exhaled. "Seventy bands."

The room got real quiet.

Then Jaylen let out a slow, knowing chuckle. "That's twice in a row." He shook his head. "You tryna start a trend, O?"

Omar's nostrils flared. "Man, that wasn't on me. That was a setup—"

"But it was your money being moved," Jaylen said smoothly. "So yeah. It was on you."

Omar's fists balled up. "Nigga, shut yo' bitch ass up."

Jaylen's smile twisted into something sharp.

"Or what?" he said, stepping forward just enough to shift the air in the room. "You gon' fight me 'cause you fumbled the bag?"

He laughed once, quick, mean.

"Nigga don't get loud now. You should've been loud when your runner got hit."

Omar just stared at Jaylen, jaw tight, sizing him up.

Jaylen let out a dry chuckle, low and cold.

"One day," he said, eyes still on Omar, "you gon' find out about me."

A.O. finally stepped forward, his tone even, but his patience wearing thin. "O, let me ask you something."

Omar met his gaze, tense.

"If this wasn't you, if this was any other nigga, what would I do?"

Omar's nostrils flared, but he didn't say shit.

Because he knew.

Everybody knew.

A.O. didn't tolerate fuckups.

But Omar? He kept getting passes.

And A.O. wasn't sure how many more he had left.

The weight in the room had shifted. Everyone was watching.

Omar stood there, jaw clenched, fists balled up at his sides, but he wasn't saying shit. Because he already knew he was in the wrong.

A.O. let the silence linger, his expression calm but unreadable. Then, he spoke.

"You embarrassing me, O. You think because you rap, because you got a name in the industry, that you untouchable?" His voice was still even, still smooth, but there was a sharp edge to it.

"Nah, nigga. Your name tied to me. You fucking up reflects on me."

Omar gritted his teeth. "I handle my shit."

A.O. cut him off. "You don't handle nothing, O. Jaylen handled that nigga in your session. Dru handled that industry nigga. Brandon and Jaylen done chase a few niggas down for you. What the fuck did you handle?

Omar held his stance, chest out, but he stayed silent.

Jaylen chuckled under his breath. "That's what I thought."

Omar snapped his head toward him. "Man, fuck you, nigga—"

"Nah, fuck you." Jaylen said, stepping forward, his voice sharper. Louder.

A.O. raised a hand, his eyes still on Omar, Jaylen stepped back. "You ain't some little nigga we just put on. You been here. You know how this works. But you keep moving sloppy.

"This your last chance."

Omar frowned, confused. "What?"

A.O. didn't repeat himself. Just leaned back slightly, eyes still on him.

"Next time you fuck up, there won't be a conversation."

He said it slow. Even.

"You'll just be out The Circle."

Omar didn't argue.

Because deep down, he already felt it.

A.O. stood still for a moment, staring at Omar like he was waiting for more, but nothing came. Just tension in the air. Then, without a word, he turned away.

He stepped toward the mirror, checking the line of his cut with a slow nod. Reached into his pocket, peeled off a few hundreds, and handed them to the barber with a quiet, "Appreciate you."

The soft clap of cash in palm was the only sound for a beat.

A.O. adjusted his cuffs, checked his watch. The room was still silent. Omar was quiet, Jaylen looked like he was ready to talk shit again but didn't. Jah stayed posted by the counter unreadable behind that poker face he wore better than anyone. The rest of the crew watched and waited.

Then the soft buzz of Apollo's phone broke the silence. He checked the screen, gave A.O. a single nod.

The front door creaked open.

Elias stepped inside like he owned the building. A tall, broad figure in a jet-black tailored suit. His salt-and-pepper beard was trimmed close, his gait steady like time bent for him. Behind him stood two men, quiet, suited muscle, but unnecessary. King didn't need protection. His name did all the work.

A.O. offered a nod as Elias approached. King had history with the family, he was tight with A.O. and Jah's father back when the Enterprise was still in its first form, a smaller, wilder version of what A.O. had built. After their father's death, A.O. had been trying to bring King back into the fold, not as a crutch, but as a calculated power move. King's product was clean. Pure. He had a direct foreign connect. And the price? Just right.

If A.O. could earn Elias's trust, and access to the connect, he could make the kind of plays that didn't just buy land, buildings, and businesses..

They bought an exit.

The two men stepped into the back, into the private room behind the barbershop, where only real business was handled. They spoke briefly, low voices, firm nods. No back and forth, no games. King didn't operate like that. If the weight moved clean, no noise, no heat, Elias would know he wasn't dealing with liabilities. Only then would he open the door to bigger drops, triple or more.

By the time A.O. returned to the main room, the crew was already posted, waiting on his word. But they didn't need much instruction. Everybody in that room was seasoned.

They already knew what time it was.

Jaylen flipped his lighter open and shut, his mind already moving numbers.

"We can push at least half through the casino. Whales and VIPs won't blink at the kind of money we're talking. No heat, no mess. We run it through the private tables, layer the drops through shell accounts, route it back through the club."

A.O. gave a slight nod.

"Keep it clean. I don't want nothing loud coming from that side."

Jaylen smirked.

"Always. They don't even know they laundering it for us."

Brandon leaned forward, sharp and efficient.

"We can take over two blocks on the west. One of the smaller crews is running light, no structure. I already sent feelers. If we move tonight, it's ours by morning. We'll run the rest of the work through there."

"We're got new field crews ready. Uber Eats and Amazon drop setups, Airbnb stash flips. Nobody sees a thing."

Deonte rubbed his chin, laid back in his chair.

"Y'all tryna flip fast. But if we stretch just a little, cut it right, keep the weight where it need to be, we double up."

Jaylen gave him a look like he'd just stepped out of a time machine.

"Nigga, this ain't the '90s. Nobody paying top dollar for stepped-on work."

Deonte shrugged, grinning like he didn't care either way.

"Just saying old tricks still work if you use 'em smart."

Dru, posted by the window, cracked his knuckles.

"I had a sit-down with a baseball exec, ready to go on at least a kilo a week & once his boys try it, we in the door with the MLB. And let me know which block's acting like they not trying to move out the way. I'll clear it out by tonight."

A.O. let them go back and forth, quiet, calculating. This was the machine.

The Black Enterprise moved like a government in the shadows. At the top was A.O., The President, rarely seen, never touched, but every move traced back to him. His Generals answered only to him, each running a critical piece of the empire: money, muscle, expansion, or protection. Beneath them were Lieutenants over zones, Captains over crews, and Sergeants who cleaned up messes before they made headlines. At the bottom were the Soldiers, ghosts in uniforms that looked like everyday life, moving weight through the city like clockwork, never asking questions, and never meeting the man they worked for.

Their foot soldiers moved like ghosts, dressed like drivers, carrying foil-wrapped bricks in fast food bags, & dropping Amazon boxes on porches so nonchalantly neighbors never suspected a thing. Airbnb stash spots rotated every few days. Real money moved through casinos, ghost kitchens, and shell companies no one would ever trace.

This was the new street work.

Clean. Controlled. Invisible.

And it was all his.

The conversation started to settle, the energy cooling just enough.

That's when Omar spoke.

"I got a play," he said, voice steady. "Music industry side."

Everyone looked up.

Jaylen raised an eyebrow, already skeptical. Jah didn't even blink. Deonte smirked.

Omar stepped forward, steady. "The label owner I told you about, he want three keys. I already got it lined up."

A.O. looked at him for a long beat. "Locked in?"

"Yeah."

Jaylen flicked his lighter once, then let it snap shut. He didn't say a word.

Jah spoke instead, calm but firm. "Every time you say that, we lose money."

Omar's jaw flexed. "I got it handled."

A.O. held up a hand, cutting the tension. "He handles it."

A.O. leaned forward, elbows on his knees, voice quiet but sharp. "Don't disappoint me."

4

The sound of kids running barefoot across the polished floors echoed through the Piersons' house. A Disney movie played in the background, too low to hear over the laughter spilling from the living room. One of the toddlers squealed, dodging a cousin's tackle. Someone had already snuck a roll off the dining table and was hiding under the stairs eating it in secret.

The kitchen was warm, golden with soft light. The scent of lamb chops sizzling in cast iron filled the house, garlicky, peppery, with a hint of rosemary from G's garden. The oven was working overtime, roasting seasoned potatoes next to a covered tray of baked mac and cheese, edges crisp and golden. Green beans simmered with smoked turkey, and the cornbread had just come out, honey-glazed and soft in the middle.

Geneva moved through it all like air, quiet,

effortless, in control. She refilled drinks, stirred the green beans, wiped stray smudges from the counter. Her smile was polite, her earrings glinting as she moved.

Perfect wife. Perfect hostess. The people at church didn't call them the Perfect Piersons for nothing, but behind the picture-perfect title, Geneva could feel the cracks.

Jah had been off.

He'd barely touched his food. Laughed at the wrong moments. Refilled his glass twice before the first course even hit the table. And he kept checking his phone under the table like he thought nobody could see him.

But she saw everything.

She always did.

She'd been seeing Jah clearly since they were barely grown, back when she got pregnant the summer after high school and he was packing to leave for college. He still went, still graduated. And for four long years, she raised the twins at her parents' house while he studied and traveled back and forth from campus to see them as much as possible.

When he finally got that first real job, he moved

them all into a home of their own. Just Jah, Geneva, and the babies they'd brought into the world too young but loved too hard to care.

He handled the money. She handled everything else.

By the time Chasiti came, they were solid. Ashanti followed, and Jah had looked her in the eye and told her, "As many as we can afford, I'll give you every one."

Three years later. The twins died.

Prom night. A rented Porsche 911. A fast turn they never came back from.

They didn't talk about it much anymore. But she still heard it in his breathing some nights. Still saw it in how quiet he got around their pictures. She'd prayed over him hard after that, joined every women's group at church, laid hands on him in his sleep, whispered scripture over his body while he tossed and turned.

But lately, it felt like whatever he was fighting was starting to win.

And Geneva wasn't the only one who noticed, but she was the first.

At the long dining table, A.O. leaned back in his chair, eyes locked on Jah as the conversation shifted toward business.

"So," A.O. said smoothly, tapping his fork against the rim of his plate. "Where we at with the lounge?"

A.O. needed the 4.5 M's for the land moved quietly, cleanly, through the only pipeline he could trust with that volume of cash without setting off alarms. Jah's hedge fund accounts. That was always Jah's value in the operation: he made dirty money look legitimate. No street-level flips, not small money for single keys. He tapped into this only when property needed to be bought, large investments need to be funded, and high ranking people needed to be bribed, real wires, real risk. But now, when A.O. needed him most, Jah was stalling. Little did he know one of the accounts were under review, flagged because he'd been shifting funds around to cover his own gambling debts. Late payments, shady transfers, he'd caused the mess himself. And now, the same accounts A.O. depended on to wash millions were too hot to touch. Jah was trying to buy time, praying A.O. wouldn't press.

Jah reached for his glass again, too fast, too casual, and took a long sip before answering. "Still moving through the final details."

A.O. lifted a brow. "That what we doing? 'Final details?"

Jah forced a chuckle, the sound thin. "Man, you act like we not about to lock it in. I got it handled."

Across the table, Geneva's fork clinked softly against her plate as she glanced at her husband again. He wouldn't meet her eyes. His jaw tightened just enough to betray the smile he tried to wear.

That was the tell.

That's what gave him away.

And then, right on cue, Jah's phone vibrated.

He exhaled through his nose, setting down his drink before checking the screen.

One glance and he pushed back his chair and stood. "Y'all keep eating. I gotta take this."

A.O. watched silently as he rounded the table and slipped out the patio door.

Jah stepped into the dry night air, phone pressed to his ear, voice low but tense. The warm night air did nothing to ease the tightness in his chest.

"I told you I need more time."

The response on the other end was sharp, cutting. Jah closed his eyes, rubbing his forehead as he listened.

Inside, his family was sitting at the dinner table. Eating, talking and laughing easy.

And out here?

He was trying to keep everything from falling apart.

The second he hung up, he exhaled, rolling his shoulders like it would shake off the weight pressing against them.

Then, he heard the door open behind him.

A.O. stepped outside, letting the screen door click shut behind him. He didn't speak at first, just slid his hands into his pockets and stared out at the perfectly manicured lawn.

Then, finally, "You wanna' tell me what that was about? I ain't never seen you leave the table during dinner, and in front of G? I can't get you to do that."

Jah chuckled under his breath, shaking his head. "Man, it's just work."

A.O. let the lie sit between them, unacknowledged.

"You slipping," he said instead, voice smooth but sharp enough to cut. "I see it. Geneva sees it." A pause. "You think nobody else does?"

Jah clenched his jaw.

"I'm good," he said, a little too fast.

A.O. turned, studying him in the dim light. "If you was good, you wouldn't be taking calls in the middle of dinner like a nigga dodging bill collectors."

Jah let out a slow breath, shaking his head. "I got it handled."

A.O. didn't look convinced.

Jah ran a hand down his face, trying to keep his tone even. "Look, you ain't gotta worry about me."

A.O. exhaled through his nose, taking a step closer. "That's where you got me fucked up, Jah." His voice was quieter now, but heavier. "I do gotta worry. 'Cause if you fall, I gotta decide whether I catch you or let you hit the ground."

Jah's stomach tightened.

A.O. studied him for another long moment before shaking his head. "Get your shit together."

Then, just like that, he turned and walked back inside.

Jah stood there alone now, phone still in his grip, his mind racing.

He wasn't about to beg A.O. for help.

That wasn't an option.

Not because A.O. wouldn't bail him out, he would, but it would come at a price. A price he wasn't willing to pay. His self-respect. His pride. His confidence in himself to stand on his own.

He wasn't asking for help.

He was fixing this.

His own way.

He opened the app, fingers flying. A few taps, a swipe, a breath he didn't realize he was holding, and it was done. A six-figure bet, placed with money he didn't have, on a stock that could make or break him by morning.

He had access to internal ledgers, temporary holds, and delayed reporting windows most people didn't understand. He knew how to shift money just long enough to place a bet and move it back before anyone noticed. It was risky as hell, but he'd done it before. This time, though, the numbers were bigger, the clock was tighter, and the market was shaky. If the stock tanked, there wouldn't be time to cover the loss, and this time, someone would notice.

With one last glance at the house behind him, Jah took a slow breath, then stepped back inside.

The smell hit him immediately, the scent of peach cobbler cooling on the counter, Chasiti was already sneaking a spoonful when she thought nobody was looking.

The low murmur of conversation filled the dining

room, laughter bubbling between sips of wine and shared plates.

A perfect family night.

And Jah was about to sit down like he wasn't one bad trade away from losing everything.

He slid back into his chair at the table, reaching for his glass like nothing had happened.

A.O. didn't say a word. Didn't even look up. Just reached for his drink with slow, deliberate ease and took a sip, eyes still on his plate. But Geneva clocked it. That subtle shift. That quiet signal.

Even he was watching.

Jah knew his brother wasn't convinced by shit he just said outside, but A.O. wasn't the one he had to worry about right now.

Geneva's eyes flicked to him over the rim of her wine glass, subtle but sharp.

Jah forced himself to meet her gaze, offering a slight smirk. "What?"

Geneva tilted her head slightly, setting her glass down with a delicate clink. "I don't know." Her voice was smooth, effortless, but the edge was there. "You tell me."

Jah kept his expression easy. "Ain't nothing to tell."

She reached for the serving spoon, casually scooping mashed potatoes onto the kids' plates, her movements calm, practiced, but he knew her too well.

She was watching.

Reading him.

Looking for cracks.

Jah picked up his fork, focusing on his food. If she ever saw anything, she wasn't about to see it tonight.

Geneva finally hummed under her breath, sipping her wine again.

But Jah knew.

She wasn't letting it go.

She never did.

And sooner or later, she was going to figure out just how deep in the hole he really was.

◆ ◆ ◆

The smell of dessert lingering in the air as the conversation drifted into familiar territory, old stories, inside jokes, and the kind of memories only family could hold onto.

Omar leaned back in his chair, one arm draped over the back, a lazy smirk on his face as he sipped from his glass. "Man, y'all remember that summer at the lake house?"

Jah chuckled under his breath, shaking his head. "Yeah, I remember you almost drowning, nigga."

Omar scoffed. "First of all, that was a jet ski malfunction."

A.O. smirked. "Nah, that was a lack of common sense."

Laughter rippled around the table. Nya nudged Omar's arm, eyes bright with amusement. "He swore he knew what he was doing too."

Omar gestured toward her, expression exaggerated. "That's crazy, because I did. I just—"

Calia raised a hand, cutting him off. "You didn't."

Even Geneva, who had been watching Jah a little too closely all night, smirked.

The conversation flowed, easy and familiar, like it always did when they were all together.

Calia and Nya teamed up, roasting Omar without mercy.

Geneva and Charlotte laughed along but still felt a little bad for him, nudging A.O. and Dru to step in and defend him.

Dru just shook his head, grinning. "That's a grown-ass man."

Omar wasn't just some tagalong in the crew.

He was family.

Omar had been there through all of it.

The wild nights, the bad decisions, the moments

that could've ended them before they had the chance to build what they had now.

A.O. might check him, Jah might clown him, but at the end of the day, Omar was still at the table.

Not because of business.

Because he belonged there.

And that was something nobody in the crew could deny.

The night had settled into a comfortable hum. The kids were in the living room, half-watching a movie, half-laughing at their own jokes. The women had migrated to the kitchen, wine glasses in hand, voices weaving between conversation and laughter.

Jah slipped back outside, the quiet settling over him like a weighted blanket. The warmth of the house felt too heavy tonight.

He needed air.

And, apparently, so did Omar.

The sliding glass door clicked shut behind him. Jah glanced back and cursed under his breath.

"Damn. The last nigga I wanna talk to right now."

Omar stepped out, hands in his pockets, posture easy, energy calm, but Jah could feel his eyes moving, clocking everything.

Jah didn't say anything at first. Just stretched his arms above his head, exhaling slow like that could somehow ease the pressure sitting on his chest.

Omar leaned against the railing, glancing at him out the corner of his eye. "You good?"

Jah smirked, shaking his head. "Nigga, do I look good?"

Omar chuckled under his breath. "You look like a nigga who just lost a bet."

Jah's smirk faded for half a second, but he covered it up, shrugging. "Nah. Just got a lot on my plate."

Omar hummed, rocking back on his heels. "A.O. on your ass?"

Jah rolled his shoulders, not confirming, not denying. "When is he not?"

That got a real laugh out of Omar.

A beat of silence stretched between them before Omar spoke again, voice lower this time. "You know, you ain't gotta do this shit alone."

Jah's jaw flexed. "Yeah, I do."

Omar studied him for a second before shaking his head. "That pride gon' kill you one day."

Jah let the words settle between them.

Omar wasn't A.O. He didn't press, didn't make shit heavier than it already was.

But he paid attention.

That was enough.

Jah exhaled, glancing toward the house where their wives were still talking, the sound of Charlotte's laugh cutting through the quiet.

"Come on," Jah said finally, nodding toward the door.

"Before they come out here looking for us."

Omar smirked. "Geneva already looking for you, nigga."

Jah chuckled, shaking his head as they headed back inside.

No matter what, Omar always made shit feel lighter.

Even when Jah knew he was sinking.

The kitchen smelled like warm vanilla and cinnamon, the last of the dessert sitting untouched on the counter while wine glasses stayed full.

Calia leaned against the island, one foot resting on the stool beneath her, her long nails tapping against the rim of her glass. "I don't know how y'all do it."

Geneva arched a brow, smirking. "Do what?"

Calia waved a hand, gesturing toward the back patio where Jah and Omar had disappeared. "Pretend like they don't drive us insane."

Charlotte let out a knowing laugh, shifting the twin

on her hip, the other fast asleep in the stroller beside her.

She and Geneva looked alike, with the same striking features, the same rich brown skin, though Charlotte was a shade lighter. Both were tall, but Charlotte was slightly shorter, with their mother's naturally curvy frame, the kind of figure that caught her NBA husband's attention when he first slid into her DMs after seeing a beach photo. Now, they shared two-year-old twin girls: Houston and Dallas.

Geneva was longer and leaner, built like the cross-country runner she'd been in high school. That's where she met Jah.

Side by side, they could've passed for paternal twins. But that's where the similarities ended.

Geneva was polished, calculated, careful.

Charlotte?

Charlotte was the wild one.

Geneva was nine years older, always playing the role of the responsible one. Charlotte and Calia had gone to school together, ran in the same circles, and back in the day?

Charlotte had been right beside Calia in the strip club, stacking money under neon lights and loud bass.

Geneva never let her forget that.

Even now, when Charlotte didn't need to work, she was making money in her own lane, social media, OnlyFans, and she wasn't apologizing for it.

Charlotte adjusted the sleeping toddler in her arms, glancing toward Calia with a smirk. "Ain't no pretending. They just lucky they fine."

Calia laughed, tilting her wine glass toward her. "That part."

Geneva scoffed, shaking her head. "Y'all are ridiculous."

Charlotte smirked. "Says the woman who's had three refills."

Geneva rolled her eyes but didn't argue.

Calia sipped her wine, shifting the conversation. "For real though, how y'all holding up? I feel like I barely see y'all outside of nights like this."

Nya sighed, twirling her glass between her fingers. "O will tell me he's 'only handling one thing today,' and then it's ten hours later."

Geneva exhaled, swirling her wine in her glass. "Jah's been distracted lately."

Charlotte's smirk faded slightly as she glanced at her sister. "Everything good?"

Geneva hesitated for a second too long.

Calia caught it immediately. "G, what's going on?"

Geneva exhaled, shaking her head. "I don't know. He's been getting more calls. Stepping away more. He says it's work, but…"

Charlotte tilted her head. "But you don't believe him."

Geneva let out a short, humorless laugh. "I've been with Jah too long to miss the signs. I just don't know what he's not telling me yet."

The moment Jah crossed the threshold back into his

home, he heard Geneva's voice.

"...He always says it's work, but if he's working so hard, why did my credit card decline twice this week.

Jah froze mid-step.

The room was quiet, too quiet.

Calia, Charlotte, and Nya all had their attention on Geneva, who was swirling the last of her wine in her glass. She hadn't noticed him yet, too caught up in her own thoughts, in her own doubts.

Charlotte tilted her head. "So do you think."

Geneva let out a short breath. "I've been with Jah too long to miss the signs. I just don't know what he's not telling me yet."

Jah clenched his jaw as he turned the corner into the kitchen.

This wasn't what he wanted to walk into.

And judging by the way Calia glanced past Geneva and locked eyes with him, she knew it too.

Geneva caught the shift, her lips parting slightly before she finally turned her head, her gaze landing on him.

The room held its breath.

Jah kept his expression smooth, raising an eyebrow. "Something I should be here for?"

Geneva didn't blink. "Depends. You got something you want to say?"

Calia immediately picked up her glass, sipping slow. Charlotte shifted the Dallas in her arms, fully invested now. Nya just exhaled, watching it unfold.

Jah smirked, stepping further into the room. "I ain't got nothing to say unless I'm actually in the conversation."

Geneva didn't flinch. "You are now."

Jah glanced at the wine bottle on the counter. "How many glasses you had?"

Geneva laughed, but it wasn't warm. "Enough to finally say what I'm thinking."

Jah's jaw flexed again, but he wasn't about to argue in front of everybody.

Instead, he reached for the whiskey bottle, pouring himself a drink. "Y'all love to stress yourselves out over nothing."

Charlotte let out a quiet "Oh, here we go."

Geneva tilted her head. "So you stepping away from dinner, taking phone calls in the middle of the night, and looking stressed every time you check your phone is nothing?"

Jah took a slow sip. "Didn't realize you was tracking my movements like that."

Geneva narrowed her eyes. "That's cute. But you know I don't miss shit."

Jah exhaled, rolling his shoulders before meeting Geneva's gaze again. He could feel the heat in her stare, the way her intuition had already figured out what he wasn't saying yet.

Geneva didn't let up. "What's going on, Jah?"

Jah swirled his drink in his glass before setting it down.

"Nothing you need to worry about."

And with that, he stepped past them and out of the kitchen.

Not a single person believed him.

5

Omar sat back, stretching his legs under the heavy conference table, watching the label exec flip through his phone before nodding at his assistant. The assistant gave a small nod back and walked out of the room.

Less than a minute later, the door reopened.

A man Omar had never seen before stepped inside, a quiet, unassuming type, dressed like he worked for the label, but with the kind of presence that said he wasn't here for music.

The exec didn't introduce him, didn't need to.

This was the guy moving the work.

Omar stayed relaxed, watching as the man walked over to the duffel bag sitting in the corner of the room. He crouched down, unzipped it, and peeled back the first kilo, pressing his thumb into the plastic wrap before nodding slightly.

"Everything's here," the man murmured, zipping the bag shut.

The exec leaned forward, clasping his hands together. "Smooth, just how I like it."

Omar smirked. "Told you."

No drama. No mistakes. Just business.

The exec gave a short nod to his guy, who lifted the bag off the floor like it held nothing. He was out the door a second later, the whole exchange lasting less than two minutes.

Omar had to give it to them. These industry niggas moved like professionals.

The exec stood up, walked to the cabinet in the corner, and opened a small safe tucked behind a speaker. He pulled out a thick envelope, unmarked, bound tight with a red rubber band, and handed it to Omar.

"All there. Count it if you want."

Omar weighed it in his palm, then tucked it into his jacket. "We good."

The exec laughed, giving him a firm handshake. "Pleasure doing business with you."

And just like that, it was done.

The keys were moved. The money was in hand. For once, Omar didn't have to call A.O. with bad news.

He stepped out into the hallway, pulled out his phone, and typed the message.

"Drop went smooth. Got the cash."

The response came seconds later.

"Meet at Omari's."

Omar locked his phone, his jaw tightening just slightly as he slid the envelope deeper into his inside pocket.

Time to face the music.

He stepped out the back of the building, the thick envelope still tucked inside his jacket, the adrenaline from the deal just starting to fade. The sun had dipped low, casting long shadows across the alley. He was halfway to his bike, helmet in hand, when he heard it—

"Yo! Omar!"

He didn't even make it to the curb.

A group of paparazzi and fans rounded the corner like they'd been waiting. Cameras flashed. A girl screamed. A man shoved a phone in his face, already recording. Another dude held out a vinyl of Omar's last album like he was begging for a signature.

Omar tensed, squinting through the flashes. "Damn..."

He threw his hood up, trying to keep moving, but they closed in fast. A couple of them were familiar, industry regulars he'd seen at shows, industry parties, but some of these faces?

He didn't recognize them.

One dude in particular stood out. Just stood back in the cut, watching. Eyes sharp. Hands in his coat pockets.

Omar's grip on the helmet tightened. He clocked the

dude, clocked the distance.

Then—

Engine purring. Tires crunching.

A lifted black Raptor R rolled to the curb, engine growling low like it had a grudge. Murdered-out paint. Blue tint. Custom wheels built for intimidation.

Jaylen.

Window down just enough to see the scowl on his face.

"You ridin' or takin' selfies, nigga?"

Omar didn't hesitate. He dodged the last flash and slid in.

The door shut. The crowd blurred behind tinted glass.

Jaylen didn't speak right away. He just pulled off smooth, one hand on the wheel, eyes straight ahead.

Omar exhaled, adjusting the envelope in his jacket. "Appreciate that."

Jaylen finally cut him a look. "You need to stop movin' like you ain't worth a hundred headlines and ten kilos."

"They popped up outta nowhere."

Omar turned back toward the road. "A.O. said meet at Omari's."

Jaylen nodded. "Already headed there."

Silence settled again, the weight of that envelope pressing into his side like a reminder.

Omar looked out the window, watching the city blur past. For a second, he could still see those cameras flashing behind his eyelids.

He was famous.

He was paid.

But he was also being watched.

And not just by the fans.

He was in too deep to slip now.

The bass thumped low through the walls, the neon glow from the stage casting everything in a mix of red and gold. The private VIP section of Omari's was tucked away from the chaos, exclusive, controlled, a space where money and power moved in silence.

A.O. sat at the center of it all, posture relaxed, presence commanding. A thick stack of money rested on the table in front of him, untouched, unbothered.

Brandon sat low in his seat, swirling his drink, eyes drifting toward the entrance between slow sips.

Deonte was off to the side, quiet, cigar in hand, gaze flicking toward the door as it opened.

Omar stepped in first, jacket half-zipped, chin high, a familiar spark in his eye. Jaylen followed right behind, giving A.O. a subtle nod, dapping up Brandon on the way in.

Deonte didn't move. Didn't speak. Just pulled slow from his cigar and kept his eyes on the table.

Omar approached and pulled a thick stack from inside his jacket, placing it on the table with a solid thump.

Jaylen stood beside him, arms crossed, casual but watchful.

A.O. didn't react at first. Just reached for his drink, took a slow sip, then finally flicked his gaze toward Jaylen.

"Count it."

Jaylen stepped forward, peeled the stack open, flipped through the bills with quick fingers, then gave a short nod. "It's all here."

Only then did A.O. glance at Omar. Cool. Measured.

"You handled it."

Omar smirked. "Told you I would."

A.O. tossed the money to Jah. "Clean it."

" This a start," he said, eyes already shifting back to Omar.

Omar's smirk faltered just slightly. "A start?"

Jaylen chuckled under his breath. "You looking for a trophy, nigga?"

Brandon cracked a small grin. "One win don't erase all them L's."

Omar opened his mouth, but Deonte leaned in just slightly, voice low, smooth.

"Let him have it," he said around his cigar. "He earned this one."

Omar cut him a glance but didn't bite. Not tonight.

A.O. picked up the money and tucked it into his coat.

"Go home, O."

Omar looked at him for a beat, jaw tight. Then he nodded once, turned, and walked out.

The club was still alive, but the VIP section had thinned out. The money had been counted, the business handled, and Omar had already walked out.

A.O. was still posted up, drinking slow, observing everything the way he always did. Jaylen and Brandon were still around, but they weren't paying attention to Deonte.

Which was fine.

Because Dru was exactly the nigga he needed to talk to next.

Deonte found him at the bar, sipping from a glass of dark liquor, his posture relaxed, his demeanor unreadable. Dru wasn't like the rest of them. He wasn't in this for money, power, or loyalty.

Dru was here because he liked hurting people.

And that?

That made him useful.

Deonte slid into the seat next to him, signaling for a drink. "I ever tell you I respect how you move?"

Dru glanced at him out the corner his eye, smirking slightly. "Nigga, you don't respect nobody."

Deonte chuckled, nodding. "True. But I get you." He leaned forward, voice dropping. "You don't need this life. You just like the power."

Dru exhaled slowly, swirling his drink. "You say that

like it's a bad thing."

Deonte smirked. "Nah. It's a dangerous thing."

Dru didn't respond right away, but he was listening.

That's all Deonte needed.

He sipped his drink before continuing, voice smooth, measured. "A.O. don't fuck with you like that."

Dru let out a short laugh. "Nigga, A.O. don't fuck with a lot of people."

Deonte tilted his head slightly. "Nah, but he really don't fuck with you. He keeps you around 'cause he knows you useful. But if you wasn't?" He shrugged. "He'd drop you like it wasn't shit."

Dru's smirk didn't fade, but his grip on the glass tightened just slightly.

Deonte leaned back, taking another sip. "A.O. think he untouchable, that's his problem. But niggas like me?" He exhaled. "I like options."

Dru finally turned his head, really looking at him now.

"You saying you got one?"

Deonte smirked. "I'm saying we both do."

Dru studied him for a beat, then chuckled under his breath. "You trying to start a war?"

Deonte shook his head. "Nah. But, a shakeup wouldn't kill nobody."

Dru didn't respond.

But he also didn't shut it down.

Which meant the seed was planted.

Deonte wasn't a reckless nigga though.

He had never been the type to move without a plan, without knowing exactly how the pieces would fall. That's why he wasn't making his move yet.

Not until A.O. gave him the opening he needed.

Dru was interested, but not committed. That was fine. Deonte had been around long enough to know that niggas like Dru didn't move just because you told them to. They needed a reason.

A.O. would give him one.

All Deonte had to do was sit back and wait.

Because every king slipped eventually.

And when A.O. did?

Deonte was going to be right there to catch the crown.

Jah sat in his home office, the glow of the computer screen reflecting in his eyes as he stared at the numbers.

For the last few hours, his heart had been sitting in his throat, every refresh of the stock chart threatening to send him spiraling.

He had made a reckless ass gamble.

And for a while, it looked like he was about to lose everything.

But now?

Now, the numbers were back in the green.

His investment wasn't just recovering, it was climbing. Fast.

Jah exhaled, running a hand over his jaw as he sat back in his chair.

All the stress, all the risk, it was paying off.

His phone buzzed on the desk.

Geneva.

He let it ring once before picking up. "Yeah?"

"Where are you?" Her voice was smooth, but he could hear the edge underneath.

"In my office."

A pause. "You coming to bed?"

Jah glanced back at the screen, watching the numbers climb a little higher.

"I'll be up in a minute."

Geneva exhaled. "Alright." She didn't sound convinced, but she didn't press.

Jah hung up, staring at the screen for another long moment before finally closing the laptop.

He had dodged the bullet.

This time.

But deep down, he knew one thing for sure.

This was not a game he could keep playing.

◆ ◆ ◆

Jah stood in the doorway of their bedroom, watching Geneva as she sat on the edge of the bed, scrolling through her phone. The glow from the screen softened her face, but he could still see the tension in her jaw, the slight furrow in her brow.

She was thinking.

Thinking too damn hard about him.

About what he wasn't saying.

Jah exhaled through his nose, stepping into the room, the air between them thick with everything unsaid.

"You still mad at me?"

Geneva didn't look up right away. "Should I be?"

Jah smirked, rubbing a hand over his beard. "I mean… I'd prefer if you weren't."

Geneva finally lifted her gaze, staring at him for a long moment before setting her phone on the nightstand. "Jahlil." Her voice was softer now, but still sharp enough to cut. "I know you. And I know when something's off."

Jah sat down next to her, reaching for her hand, but she pulled away slightly. Not enough to be a rejection, but just enough to let him know she wasn't letting this go yet.

He sighed, leaning forward, resting his elbows on his knees. "I got a lot on my plate right now. That's it."

Geneva tilted her head. "And that's supposed to be enough for me?"

Jah turned his head toward her, eyes locked onto

hers. "For now? Yeah."

Geneva scoffed, shaking her head, her lips pressing into a thin line. "Jah, I'm your wife. You don't get to shut me out when shit gets heavy."

Jah dragged a hand over his face. "I'm not shutting you out, G. I'm handling shit."

Geneva let out a slow breath, her gaze softening just a little. "You don't have to handle everything alone."

Jah chuckled dryly. "Yeah, I do."

Geneva stared at him, and for a moment, it was quiet.

She knew Jah.

Knew how he moved, how he carried everything on his back until it damn near broke him.

And she hated it.

She shifted closer, reaching for his hand, lacing their fingers together. "I don't care how much money you make. If you lose yourself trying to keep it, it's not worth it."

Jah's jaw flexed. "I ain't losing myself."

Geneva gave him a look. "Then stop acting like you are."

Jah exhaled slowly, his thumb brushing over the back of her hand. "You really not gonna let this go, huh?"

Geneva smirked slightly. "Nope."

Jah let out a low chuckle, shaking his head before pulling her onto his lap. "You always gotta challenge me, don't you?"

Geneva wrapped her arms around his neck, her lips grazing his jaw. "Somebody has to."

Jah sighed, leaning into her warmth, his fingers slipping beneath the silk of her nightgown. "Let me make it up to you."

Geneva hummed, tilting her head slightly. "Oh, now you wanna make it up to me?"

Jah smirked, his lips finding hers. "Gotta keep my wife happy."

Geneva kissed him back, slow and deep, melting into him as his hands slid down her back, pulling her closer.

For the rest of the night, Jah let himself forget.

Forget the calls.

Forget the numbers.

Forget the pressure.

Because right now, this was all that mattered.

And as long as Geneva still let him hold her like this...

Maybe he hadn't lost her yet.

The studio was dim, the only light coming from the glow of the mixing board and the soft flicker of the neon sign above the door. The bass from the track playing through the speakers thumped low, but Omar wasn't listening.

He was pissed.

He had stood on business. He had brought the money in, clean, smooth, no drama.

And still?

It wasn't enough.

A.O. barely acknowledged it. The rest of them treated it like some small-ass accomplishment, like he should be grateful just to have a seat at the table.

Omar took a slow sip from the glass in his hand, the liquor burning its way down his throat.

What more did they want from him?

The door to the lounge cracked open, and a soft voice slipped through the heavy air.

"Knew I'd find you here."

He didn't have to look up.

Sienna.

Her eyes drifted toward his screen. "You working on something new?"

He nodded, rubbing the back of his neck. "Trying. Shit ain't clicking, though."

She crossed the room and leaned over the desk, her perfume, warm vanilla mixed with something dangerously sweet, floating in the air between them. "Let me hear it."

Omar hesitated, then tapped the space bar.

The beat played, a moody, haunting loop layered with heavy drums and soft strings. Sienna closed her eyes for a second, letting it wash over her.

"Damn," she murmured. "You made this?"

He nodded. "Started it last week. Been trying to find the right drop, but it keeps slipping."

She tilted her head, listening. "It don't sound like the usual shit you do."

He shrugged. "I've been in my head lately."

Sienna didn't respond at first. She walked over to the small bar cart in the corner and poured herself a drink. "Stress'll do that." She sipped, then leaned against the wall. "You good?"

The beat looped again, soft now, like background noise to the moment stretching between them.

He glanced at her.

Her eyes were on him.

Not hungry. Not obvious.

Just open.

Omar exhaled. "You tryna stay for a bit?"

She smiled, soft and slow. "That depends. You letting me?"

He nodded.

She poured another drink.

They didn't talk much after that. Just drank. Listened. Talked about sound design, old-school albums, the way drums hit different when you layer them with vinyl crackle. Omar showed her a few tricks on the board, and Sienna leaned in close, her laugh light, her attention easy and unforced.

He didn't mean to let his guard down.

But somewhere between the beat and the burn of the liquor, he stopped fighting it.

Her hand brushed his.

Then her thigh.

Then her lips.

Soft. Slow.

It didn't feel calculated.

It felt like falling.

Like slipping off the edge of something you already knew was there.

Her fingers trailed up his arm, slow and deliberate, her nails barely grazing his skin. "You always this tense?"

Omar smirked, but it didn't reach his eyes. "You always this persistent?"

She smiled, tilting her head slightly, studying him like she already knew the answer. "Only when I see something worth chasing."

Omar's grip on his glass tightened, his jaw clenching for a second before he exhaled. "Yea?"

She nodded, shifting closer, the scent of her wrapping around him, warm and sweet, dangerously inviting.

Omar's heart pounded harder than it should.

He had no business sitting here, letting this moment become something else.

But he was tired.

Tired of fighting for a spot he should already have. Tired of proving himself to niggas who still looked at him like he didn't belong.

And maybe for just one night, he wanted to stop caring.

She placed her glass on the table, her fingers slipping beneath his chin, tilting his head toward her. "You think too much."

Omar smirked, but this time, it was lazy, hazy, the kind that came when you stopped giving a fuck.

"Yeah?"

She nodded, leaning in, lips brushing his jaw first, slow, deliberate, testing.

He didn't stop her.

Didn't flinch.

Didn't think.

But just before their lips met, a flicker of Nya's face cut through his mind, her tired smile, the way she curled up with Alya, the way she always knew when he was spiraling, even when he tried to hide it.

But when her lips finally pressed against his, soft and coaxing, he pressed back.

The music was still playing, but it sounded distant now, like even the beat knew he'd gone too far.

The moment stretched, turned into something heavier, something reckless.

Hands tangled in fabric, movements slow at first, then rushed.

Heat pressed between them, her soft sighs, his heavy breaths, the sound of regret forming before it even settled.

Omar knew this was wrong.

But at this moment?

He didn't care.

Not until it was over.

Not until the room was silent again, and the weight of what he'd just done crushed him all at once.

His stomach twisted as he leaned back, his head resting against the couch, his breathing still uneven.

She shifted beside him, the same knowing smile playing on her lips as she reached for the bottle again.

Omar ran a hand down his face, guilt creeping in like a slow-moving poison.

He had fucked up.

And now?

He had to live with it.

6

The house was quiet.

The kind of stillness that only settled when the rest of the world was asleep.

Jah moved carefully, slipping out of bed without disturbing Geneva. He didn't look back at her.

Couldn't.

Instead, he grabbed his phone, his keys, and his bad habits, sliding out the front door into the cool night air.

His car was already running when he settled into the driver's seat. Music low, one hand on the wheel, the other tapping restlessly against his thigh as he drove.

The farther he got from home, the heavier the weight in his chest became.

He shouldn't be doing this.

But at the same time?

He couldn't stop himself.

The lot was empty except for a single blacked-out Escalade parked deep in the shadows. The streetlights barely touched it, like even the city didn't want to acknowledge what went down here.

Jah pulled in slow, stomach tightening as he rolled to a stop.

A man leaned against the hood of the SUV, arms crossed, posture casual, but nothing about this was casual.

Jah exhaled through his nose and stepped out.

The man smirked, tilting his head. "Mr. Pierson. Wasn't sure I was gonna see you tonight."

Jah didn't answer. Just reached into his pocket and pulled out a thick stack of cash. Held it out. Tight.

"We square?"

The man flipped through the bills slowly before nodding. "For now."

Jah let out a slow breath. "Good." He turned, ready to walk away.

"You callin' it a night already?" The man's voice was smooth. Knowing. "That ain't your style."

Jah should've kept walking. Should've gotten in his car and gone home.

Instead, he hesitated.

And that was all the man needed.

He chuckled, shaking his head. "I know why you here. You don't come out in the middle of the night just to settle a debt. You come because you want more."

Jah's pulse pounded in his ears.

He swallowed. "I'm good."

The man smirked. "You sure?"

Jah wasn't sure of shit.

Twenty minutes later, he wasn't in his car driving home.

He was sitting in a private high-stakes game, cards in hand, heart racing, chasing something he'd never be able to catch.

Because this?

This was the real problem.

Not one bad bet. Not one reckless decision.

A pattern.

A hunger that had nothing to do with money, and everything to do with the high.

His hands were steady as he placed his next bet.

His mind told him to walk away.

But his body was already leaning in.

Because win or lose?

The rush was the same.

And that was the part he was really chasing.

◆ ◆ ◆

The air in the private lounge was thick with cigar smoke and bad decisions.

Stacks of cash lined the table. Chips clinked. Hands dealt. Bets placed.

Men chasing that feeling that kept them coming back.

Jah was locked in, eyes sharp, every move calculated.

This was where he thrived.

Where pressure was the drug. Where risk gave him a high money couldn't buy.

And tonight?

He was winning.

Hand after hand. Bet after bet. His stack kept growing.

The other players noticed, some irritated, some impressed.

Jah barely noticed them at all.

All he saw were numbers rising.

The rush building.

The weight in his chest finally easing.

He was back in control.

The dealer slid another card toward him. Jah tapped his knuckles against the felt. Hold.

The last bet was placed.

Cards flipped.

He won.

A pot so heavy it should've been enough.

Enough to clear the rest of his debts.

Enough to walk away.

But the rush was still there.

That itch.

That feeling in his bones telling him he could keep it going.

One more hand.

Just one.

Jah leaned forward, tapping the table. "Run it back."

The room felt electric.

His stack sat heavy in front of him, more money than most people made in a year.

He should've walked away.

He knew that.

But that wasn't how this worked.

The rush was thrumming in his veins.

Hands steady as he reached for another stack.

The dealer shuffled. Cards hit the table.

Jah smirked. Leaned in.

"All in."

A murmur rippled through the other players.

Some shook their heads.

Others just watched.

The dealer nodded. "Bets locked."

The game moved fast.

Too fast.

Time blurred until the final card dropped.

And then.

Jah's stomach dropped with it.

The other player laid down a hand that beat his by one card.

Jah's smirk froze. Then faded.

The dealer exhaled, pushing the pot across the table, away from him.

Gone.

All of it.

But that wasn't even the worst part.

He had bet beyond what he had.

He owed.

A lot.

And the man who had just taken his money?

He was staring at Jah like he already knew how this was going to end.

Jay swallowed hard.

He had just fucked up.

Bad.

Jah kept his face still.

Movements calm.

Expression unreadable.

He had just lost everything.

More than everything, money he didn't even have.

And now?

He had to walk out like it was nothing.

The man across the table watched him, waiting for panic.

He pushed back from the table, exhaled slow. Rolled his shoulders.

Like this was just another game.

He pulled out his phone, checked the time like he was bored. "I'll be in touch."

The house was quiet when Omar stepped inside.

The kind of stillness that only came in the late hours

of the night.

The scent of lavender and baby powder lingered in the air, a stark contrast to the liquor and smoke still clinging to his clothes.

He shouldn't be here feeling like this.

Not after where he'd just been.

Not after what he'd just done.

Omar exhaled slowly, setting his keys down on the kitchen counter, his hands flexing at his sides.

He needed a shower.

Needed to wash the scent of another woman off him before he climbed into bed next to his wife.

Before he kissed their daughter goodnight like nothing had happened.

A soft voice cut through his thoughts. "You're late."

Omar turned toward the hallway, his chest tightening at the sight of her.

Nya stood just outside the nursery, dressed in one

of his old t-shirts, her long hair falling over her shoulders.

Barefoot. Relaxed.

But her eyes?

Sharp. Watching him.

Omar forced a smirk. "Studio ran over."

Nya folded her arms, tilting her head slightly. "That right?"

He nodded too quickly. "Yeah. Just lost track of time."

She hummed, unconvinced.

Then pushed off the doorframe, walking toward him slow. Her gaze never left his.

"You smell like Hennessy."

Omar chuckled, rubbing a hand over his beard. "You saying I can't have a drink?"

Nya stopped in front of him, close enough that he could smell the faint vanilla on her skin.

"You can do whatever you want, O."

She tilted her head, voice softer now. "I just wanna know why you look like you got something to hide."

Omar swallowed hard, forcing himself not to flinch.

She had always been able to read him too well.

And tonight?

She was looking at him like she already knew.

He shook his head, reaching for her waist, pulling her against him. "Come on. You really wanna fight with me this late?"

Nya didn't push him away.

Her voice was quiet when she finally spoke.

"You sure there's nothing you need to tell me?"

Omar kissed her forehead, lingering longer than he should have.

"I'm sure."

A lie.

One that settled heavy in his chest.

A soft whimper came from the nursery, breaking the moment.

Nya glanced over her shoulder. "She's been restless all night."

Omar exhaled, relieved for the excuse to step away. "I'll go check on her."

She didn't stop him.

Didn't say a word as he walked past her into the nursery.

But he could still feel her eyes on his back.

Still feel the weight of his mistake, pressing down harder than before.

The morning sun filtered through the curtains, casting a soft glow across the bedroom.

Nya stirred first, stretching beneath the sheets, half-aware of the warmth beside her.

Except, for once, Omar wasn't still in bed.

She frowned slightly, turning her head just as the scent of fresh-brewed coffee and something sweet drifted into the room.

That was new.

Omar didn't cook.

At least, not like this.

Nya pushed the covers back, slipping out of bed and padding into the kitchen, then paused at the sight in front of her.

Omar stood at the stove, shirtless, sweatpants hanging low on his hips, flipping pancakes like this was something he did every day.

Alya sat in her high chair, happily smacking her hands against the tray, little curls bouncing as she babbled.

The whole scene looked too perfect.

Too intentional.

Nya leaned against the doorway, arms crossing over her chest. "You wanna tell me why you're acting like husband of the year this morning?"

Omar turned slightly, flashing a grin. "Damn. God forbid a man cook for his family without it being suspicious?"

Nya raised a brow. "You? Cooking breakfast? On a random Tuesday morning? Yeah, I'm suspicious."

He chuckled, flipping the last pancake onto a plate. "Maybe I just wanted to do something nice for my girls."

Nya didn't respond right away, just watched as he moved toward Alya, wiping a stray bit of syrup off her chin.

Omar was good with their daughter.

Better than she'd even expected. Always present. Always patient.

That part?

She never questioned.

But this?

This was forced.

She stepped forward, grabbing a piece of fruit from the plate on the counter. "You are overcompensating for something, O?"

Omar smirked, but his hands tensed slightly where they rested on the highchair.

"Nope." He leaned in, pressing a quick kiss to her lips before nudging a plate toward her. "Eat."

Nya held his gaze for another long second before finally grabbing a fork.

Jah sat at his desk, fingers hovering over the keyboard, his pulse pounding in his ears.

This was a bad idea.

He knew it.

But right now?

He didn't have any other options.

The numbers from last night's game were still burned into his brain, the reality of what he owed sitting heavy in his chest. He had barely slept, lying next to Geneva with his mind racing through every possible way to fix this before it spiraled.

And this?

This was the only move he could make without raising alarms.

For now.

Jah exhaled, clicking through his company's internal banking system, eyes scanning the list of accounts under his management.

Billions in assets.

Millions moving in and out every day.

He'd already been cleaning money for TBE through these pipelines, moving bribe money, laundering drops, skimming small amounts here and there when it made sense.

But this?

This was different.

This was personal.

Riskier.

He wasn't stealing.

Not really.

He just needed to borrow enough to cover himself, just until he flipped it back.

He'd done it before.

He could do it again.

His fingers moved quickly, transferring a six-figure sum from one of the discretionary investment accounts and shifting it into an off-book holding. Nothing too obvious. Nothing that would set off immediate red flags.

The confirmation popped up.

He exhaled slowly, sitting back in his chair.

Done.

Now he just had to replace it before anyone noticed.

His phone vibrated.

A text from the man he owed.

"I'll be expecting you soon. Don't keep me waiting."

7

The midday sun streamed through the studio's high windows, cutting across the sleek black floors. The smell of coffee still lingered in the air, mixing with the faint hum of the monitors as Omar sat behind the mixing board, trying to focus.

Trying to forget.

But his mind wasn't in it.

No matter how many times he ran the track back, no matter how many adjustments he made, all he could hear was his own heartbeat pounding in his ears.

Last night.

Sienna.

The way he let himself slip.

Omar inhaled deeply, shaking his head like it would clear the memory from his mind. It was done. Over.

Now, he just needed to act normal.

Jaylen sat on the couch behind him, scrolling through his phone. "Nigga, you been tweaking that same mix for an hour. Either it's good, or you don't know what the fuck you doing."

Omar exhaled sharply. "I know what I'm doing."

Jaylen smirked, stretching his arms behind his head. "Then hurry the fuck up. I got shit to do."

Omar was about to respond, but then—

The door cracked open.

Sienna stepped in like she belonged there.

Moving through the studio like it was hers, like walking in unannounced wasn't a problem.

Omar's stomach dropped.

Jaylen's head lifted slightly, his sharp gaze flicking between Sienna and Omar.

She smiled, slow and easy. "Knew I'd find you here."

Omar's jaw clenched.

Fuck.

Jaylen sat up, eyebrows raised. "Who the fuck is this?"

Omar moved too fast. "Jay, step out for a second."

Jaylen's smirk disappeared. "What?"

Omar was already standing, too tense, too obvious. "Just give me a minute."

Jaylen's gaze returned to Sienna, who stood with the calm of someone waiting for something she already knew would come.

Jaylen exhaled through his nose. "Nigga, you trippin'."

Omar's jaw flexed. "Jay."

A beat passed. Then Jaylen let out a dry chuckle.

"Aight."

He pushed up from his seat, shooting Sienna one last look before stepping out of the room.

The door clicked shut behind Sienna and Jaylen, leaving just the two of them.

Omar exhaled, rubbing a hand over his face before meeting her gaze. "You can't pop up like that."

Sienna smirked, unbothered. "Why not?"

He shot her a look. "You know why."

She stepped closer, head tilting. "So last night was what? A mistake?"

Omar's jaw tightened. "Yeah."

Sienna hummed, folding her arms. "Didn't feel like one."

Omar held her stare. "I can't do that again. Let's just be cool."

She studied him for a beat before shrugging. "If you say so."

But the way she said it, like she didn't believe him. Like he didn't even believe himself.

He ran a hand over his face, keeping his voice steady. "Look, I'm serious. I got a family. A wife. This ain't me."

Sienna raised a brow, her smirk lingering. "It was last night."

Omar gritted his teeth. "Sienna."

She laughed softly, shaking her head. "Relax, O. I ain't here to start no problems."

He exhaled, his shoulders loosening slightly. "Good. "

She pulled out her phone, unlocked the screen, and held it out for him. "Well, if we're going to be just friends for real."

Omar hesitated.

He knew better.

But she stood there, waiting, watching, like she already knew what he was gonna do.

He pulled out his phone.

Numbers were exchanged.

No words.

Nothing needed to be said.

Sienna tucked her phone away, smirking one last time before heading for the door.

The door clicked shut.

Omar exhaled, rolling his shoulders like he could shake off the weight settling in his chest.

This was getting messy.

He needed to lock in.

Move smart.

But before he could even process his next step.

The door swung back open.

Jaylen stepped inside and shut the door slow but firm behind him.

Jaylen slid his phone into his pocket, nodding toward the door. "Who was that?"

Omar grabbed a water bottle off the desk, twisting the cap slow. "Nobody."

Jaylen smirked. "Yeah? You clearing the room for nobodies now? Got me stepping out like some goofy nigga, and she in here moving like she got rank with you."

Omar didn't answer, just took a slow sip, his expression blank.

"It's nothin'."

Jaylen exhaled through his nose, watching him. "You sure? 'Cause I pillow talk with your Nya's cousin every night, and I'd hate to hear something foul through her before I hear it from you."

Omar clenched his jaw. "You trippin'."

Jaylen let the silence stretch before shaking his head, smirking. "Aight, bet."

Omar exhaled, tossing the water bottle onto the desk. "Nigga, you got something to say, say it."

Jaylen shrugged. "Nah, I'ma let you tell it when you ready."

Then, he turned and walked out.

The Escalade rolled smooth up the long-gated driveway, sunlight bouncing off its polished black hood. Jah exhaled through his nose, glancing at the rearview mirror.

The kids were already acting up in the back, feet kicking against seats, arguing over the iPad even though they all had one..

To them?

This wasn't business.

This was Uncle A.O.'s house.

He parked near the front steps, tossing the SUV in park.

"Aye, listen, don't be running all through they house," Jah said, cutting off the ignition. "Y'all hear me?"

Chasiti crossed her arms like always. "We know, Daddy."

Jah chuckled. "We gon' see."

The second he unlocked the doors, the triplets burst out first, shoes slapping against the pavement as they raced toward the house like they owned it.

Ashanti climbed out slower, hand still wrapped around Chasiti's, talking her ear off about some cartoon they'd been watching on the way.

Inside, the house was quiet except for the echo of little feet and excited voices.

Malia was in her bouncer near the living room, squealing with joy the moment she saw the chaos coming her way.

The triplets crowded around her instantly, making baby faces and grabbing for her little fingers. Chasiti and Ashanti followed more chill, but just as soft when it came to their baby cousin.

A.O. was leaning in the doorway, watching.

Not saying much.

Just watching.

For a second, Jah caught the soft shift in his brother's face.

It wasn't a smile. Not really.

But it was close.

Something warm flickered when Malia reached up toward Chasiti, her little fingers curling in the air.

Jah stepped forward, smirking. "Didn't know you was hosting a daycare today."

A.O. finally looked over, shaking his head. "Long as they don't break shit, we cool."

Jah raised a brow. "I ain't making no promises."

A.O. stepped forward, his energy shifting the second he entered the room.

The triplets straightened up immediately.

Even Chasiti, who barely paid attention to *Jah* on a good day, stood taller, eyes on her uncle like he was royalty.

A.O. crouched slightly, voice calm but firm. "Y'all listening?"

A chorus of small voices responded: "Yes, Uncle A.O."

He nodded. "Aight. Y'all in my house now. Act like y'all got some sense."

They nodded, wide-eyed.

Jah laughed. "Damn, nigga. They don't even listen to me like that."

A.O. stood, unfazed. "That's 'cause yo ass soft."

"Nigga, fuck you," Jah said, grinning.

A.O. smirked but didn't fire back.

Instead, he let his eyes settle on Jah.

And just like that, the energy shifted again, subtle but real.

"Come outside."

Jah let out a breath, rubbing his jaw. "What now?"

A.O. turned toward the patio doors. "Just talkin'."

◆ ◆ ◆

The backyard was quiet, sunlight cutting across the stone patio in long, lazy streaks. Jah stepped out behind A.O., his pace easy, posture relaxed. This wasn't a sit-down. Not yet. Just a Talk.

A.O. didn't say anything at first. Just moved toward the edge of the yard like he was checking the landscaping.

Jah glanced back through the glass, watching the kids tumble into the den. "They always that good when you talk?"

A.O. gave a short chuckle. "Nigga, they just know I ain't the one to play with."

Jah smirked, shaking his head. "Wish that shit worked at my house."

They let the silence settle for a moment, the only

sound coming from birds chirping in the trees and the faint laughter of children inside.

Then A.O. asked.:

"You been paying attention to Deonte?"

Jah blinked, caught off guard. Deonte?

He was quiet. Old school. The kind of nigga who'd been around so long, you stopped watching him.

If A.O. wanted eyes on him now... that meant something had changed.

Jah tilted his head. "Wasn't he the one that put you on?"

A.O. turned his face up, like the question offended him. "Nigga, Pops put me under him back in the day. That was his move. I didn't pick that nigga."

A.O. looked away for a second, watching the trees sway. "I don't trust him."

That landed hard. Not loud. But definite.

Jah's face didn't change, but he let the silence speak for a second.

"You think he making moves?"

"I think he's waiting," A.O. said quietly.

That was worse.

Because a man moving could be stopped.

Jah nodded slowly. "You want me to start watching him?"

A.O. didn't answer directly. Just said, "He was running his mouth in the club... slick shit. 'What if somebody else was in my seat, that type of shit."

Jah's jaw tightened. "He wild for that."

A.O. turned toward him again, posture calm. "Just keep your eyes open"

Jah gave a sharp nod. "I got you."

A beat passed.

Then A.O. shifted gears like he'd never brought it up.

"Now let's talk about this lounge."

Jah groaned. "You mean the one I ain't even had time to finalize yet?"

A.O. smirked, slow and deliberate. "Nigga, I already pulled the trigger on it."

Jah blinked. "What the fuck?"

"You was moving too slow," A.O. said simply.

"That was supposed to be my call," Jah muttered.

"Was it?" A.O. tilted his head.

Jah's jaw tensed, but then A.O. added—

"This one feel different. Like it could actually be the way out. Real legit wealth. Not a front. Not a wash. This the kind of shit I can build out and walk away with my lifestyle untouched."

Jah studied him for a beat, then nodded, slipping back into his role.
"I'll scope the landscape. Soon as I can move it, I will."

A.O. smirked again, not saying a word at first. Just watching him.

"You gon' move it, huh?"

Jah chuckled. "Why you say it like that?"

"'Cause I know you," A.O. said. His voice wasn't sharp, just knowing.

Jah kept his tone light. "And?"

A.O. took a slow sip from his water bottle. "And you better not bullshit me."

Jah forced a smile. Swallowed a little tighter than usual.

He nodded. "You know I'ma handle it."

A.O. let the silence stretch before giving him a final nod.

Jah turned, glancing toward the house, listening to the muffled sounds of the kids playing.

And as he stepped off the patio and back toward the noise of family and routine...

8

The restaurant was classy without trying too hard. Dim lights, low jazz, and thick white tablecloths that whispered money.

Omar adjusted his watch as he followed the hostess, Nya's hand resting lightly on his arm.

This was supposed to be a reset.

A night to focus on Nya.

To remind himself that he had something solid.

That he had no business slipping.

Jaylen and Alisha were already at the table when they arrived.

Jaylen was leaned back, relaxed as hell, one arm

draped around Alisha like he had nothing to prove.

Alisha flipped through the cocktail menu like she already knew she was getting two.

The moment she saw Nya, she lit up. "Finally! Thought y'all were gonna stand us up."

Nya laughed as Omar pulled out her chair. "Girl, you know Omar takes forever to tie up his locs."

Omar smirked his freeforms tied up expertly. "Nah, she just needed two hours for her everything shower."

Jaylen chuckled, eyes still on Alisha. "Yeah, I'm on Nya side, nigga."

Alisha leaned into Jaylen, gold anklet glinting under the table, her loose curls brushing his shoulder as she flipped the menu toward him. "Baby, what you think?"

"Both," Jaylen said, barely glancing.

She giggled, her diamond nose stud catching the candlelight. "You just tryna get me drunk."

"Maybe." His fingers traced circles on her shoulder.

Omar shook his head. "Nigga, she got you wrapped."

Jaylen shrugged. "And?"

Alisha smirked, the kind of smirk that made you forget she looked so sweet. "Aww, look at you. Acting soft."

"Only for you," Jaylen murmured, lacing their fingers together.

Omar chuckled, but something about the moment stuck with him.

His phone buzzed in his pocket.

Sienna.

Sienna: O... really?

Sienna: You just gone sit there like I don't exist?

Sienna: Wow. Bet.

Sienna: Answer your phone.

Omar's jaw clenched. He shifted in his seat, fingers tightening around his glass.

Nya was laughing at something Alisha said.

Jaylen was brushing his thumb over Alisha's hand.

Nobody was watching him.

This was his chance.

Omar cleared his throat. "I'ma hit the bathroom real quick."

Nya glanced up. "You good?"

He forced a smirk. "Yeah, just gimme a sec."

He didn't wait for a response, just grabbed his phone and walked off, heart pounding loud in his ears.

Omar stepped into the bathroom, the door clicking shut behind him.

Gold fixtures. Soft lighting. Marble counters. The kind of upscale setup that felt more like a hotel than a restaurant.

He checked the stalls.

Empty.

He pulled out his phone, jaw tight as he hit call.

Sienna answered before the first ring even finished.

"Took you long enough."

Omar gritted his teeth. "Sienna, what the fuck is wrong with you?"

She laughed, soft and slow, like this was some kind of game. "Relax, O. You act like I'm the problem."

Omar lowered his voice, glancing at the door. "You are."

"You sure about that?"

His pulse ticked.

She was playing with him.

Like she knew he couldn't move how he wanted.

Like she knew he was stuck.

Omar rubbed a hand down his beard, exhaling hard.

"I'm out with my wife. That mean stop fucking texting me."

Sienna hummed, unbothered. "And whose fault is that?"

Omar gritted his teeth. "This shit stops now."

Sienna clicked her tongue. "Oh, so now you done?"

Omar's stomach twisted.

He was about to respond when the door creaked open behind him.

Jaylen stepped inside, catching everything in one glance.

Omar turned his back slightly, lowering his voice. "I'ma call you back."

He hung up too fast.

Too obvious.

Jaylen took a slow step forward, his voice dropping.

"I ain't here to tell you what to do," he muttered. "But I'ma tell you this, once Nya finds out? That's it."

Omar's throat tightened.

Jaylen rubbed a hand over his beard. "And she will find out."

Omar scoffed, shaking his head. "Nigga, I got it handled."

Jaylen let out a humorless chuckle. "Yeah? That's why you hiding in the bathroom?"

Omar clenched his fists, his body going tight.

Jaylen clicked his tongue, shaking his head. "Damn, O. You really lettin' a bitch like that fuck up your whole life?"

Omar's jaw tensed. "Nigga, I told you, mind your business."

Jaylen smirked. "I mean, I get it. She look good. But she ain't 'fuck up my whole marriage' good."

Omar exhaled sharply, rubbing a hand down his face.

Jaylen's smirk widened. "You want me to handle that?"

Omar's head snapped toward him. "Nigga, what?"

Jaylen shrugged. "You want her gone, don't you? Say the word."

Omar stared at him.

Because the way Jaylen said it?

It wasn't a joke.

Jaylen tilted his head. "You too sloppy to clean it up yourself. I could make sure she don't even remember your name."

Omar's pulse ticked. "Jaylen. Chill."

Jaylen smirked, but his tone didn't change. "You sure? 'Cause she blowing you up like she got a reason to."

Omar clenched his jaw. "I got it handled."

Jaylen let the silence stretch, then finally shrugged. "Aight."

He pushed off the wall, stepping toward the door. "But when you don't? Don't say I ain't try to help."

Then he walked out.

Omar stayed there, his pulse still uneven.

Because as much as he wanted to believe Jaylen was just talking shit...

He knew better.

And if it ever got to that point?

Jaylen wouldn't hesitate.

◆ ◆ ◆

The house was warm, quiet, the kind of stillness that came late at night, when the world slowed down, when nothing else mattered except what was in front of you.

Omar let out a slow breath, watching as Nya kicked off her heels, stretching out her arms, rolling her neck.

She looked good.

Too good.

And the guilt?

It was eating him alive.

She turned to him, head tilted. "You've been quiet since we left the restaurant."

Omar forced a smirk, stepping forward, his hands finding her waist. "Just thinking."

Nya narrowed her eyes. "About what?"

Omar didn't answer.

Instead, he kissed her.

Because words weren't gonna fix this.

Only this.

Only them.

She melted into him, pulling him closer, pulling him back into what they were before all this bullshit.

He let her.

He let himself believe, for a moment, that he could

erase everything.

That this moment could cover the mess he had made.

They made it to the bedroom in a blur of touches, of hushed whispers, of need.

Nya clung to him like she always did. Like he was hers.

And for the first time in a long time?

Omar wanted to believe it.

But even as they moved together, even as she pulled him deeper, that gnawing guilt sat in his chest.

That voice whispering in the back of his mind.

You don't deserve this.

Omar was knocked out, his arm heavy over Nya's waist, his breathing slow and steady.

But Nya?

She was wide awake.

Something wasn't sitting right.

Something about tonight. About Omar's energy. About the way Jaylen was acting.

And then—

She saw it.

His phone.

Buzzing.

Again.

Her stomach tightened.

Slowly, carefully, she reached for it, her heart already pounding.

She knew she shouldn't.

She knew she wasn't gonna like what she found.

But she did it anyway.

And the second she unlocked it.

The second she saw the texts.

Everything shattered.

Sienna: You up?

Sienna: I'm sorry, I miss you.

Sienna: You can't ignore me forever, baby.

Nya's breath caught.

Her hands shook as she scrolled, scanning the thread, messages that made her stomach turn.

She felt sick.

She felt stupid.

Omar stirred beside her, shifting, pulling her close in his sleep like he had no worries.

Like he wasn't out here embarrassing her.

A sharp rage clawed its way up her throat.

She sat up so fast the bed shifted beneath her.

Omar's breathing hitched. He blinked, groggy. "What's wrong?"

Nya's voice shook. "Who the fuck is Sienna?"

Omar's entire body locked up.

Too slow.

Too late.

The phone hit his chest before she was on her feet, pacing, her entire body trembling.

"I swear to God, Omar, tell me I'm trippin'."

Omar sat up fast, hands already up, voice low. "Nya, listen—"

"No, nigga! You listen!" Her voice cracked, rage and betrayal pouring out all at once. "I trusted you, I loved you, and the whole time—"

She couldn't even finish.

Her chest was too tight.

Her vision blurred.

Omar swung his legs over the bed, standing slowly, carefully, like he was approaching something fragile. "Baby, it's not—"

"Don't fucking touch me!"

His hands dropped immediately.

Silence.

Thick. Suffocating.

Then—

Nya pointed at the door.

"Get out."

Omar's stomach dropped. "Nya—"

"Now, Omar."

The studio was dim. Quiet.

Omar had been driving for hours, no destination, his thoughts looping with no way out.

He had fucked up.

He had nothing.

No home. No wife. No fucking clue what to do next.

He pushed the door open, ready to drink, smoke, anything to silence the noise in his head.

But then?

She was there.

Sienna.

Sitting on the couch like she belonged there.

Like she'd been waiting.

Like she already knew he'd come.

She smirked, tilting her head. "Rough night?"

Omar's jaw clenched.

He should leave.

Should turn around and walk out.

But instead?

He shut the door.

Because tonight?

He had nothing left to lose.

Omar woke up to silence.

A heavy, suffocating kind of silence that settled deep in his chest before he even opened his eyes.

His head was pounding. His body stiff.

The sheets were too soft. The room smelled different, vanilla and something dangerously sweet.

Then it hit him.

This wasn't home.

This wasn't Nya's bed.

His stomach dropped.

He turned his head slowly.

Sienna.

Fast asleep, curled under the sheets, her long hair spilling over the pillow.

Omar's throat went dry.

What the fuck did he do?

His phone buzzed on the nightstand.

Then again.

And again.

He reached for it, his chest tightening the second he saw the screen.

Missed calls.

Texts.

Flooded.

Jaylen: Nigga, where you at?

Calia: Omar, please tell me this isn't true.

A.O.: Call me. Now.

Geneva: Wow, nigga.

Nothing from Nya.

And that silence?

That hurt the worst.

Omar rubbed a hand down his face, pulse hammering.

His whole life was falling apart.

And Sienna?

She just stretched, sighing softly, completely unbothered.

Like she had won.

Like she already knew he wasn't leaving.

And the fucked-up part?

She might be right.

He sat up in bed, heart pounding, and dialed Nya's number.

One ring.

Two.

Then—

Voicemail.

He tried again.

Straight to voicemail.

"Fuck."

His fingers moved fast.

Omar: Nya, please. Just talk to me.

Omar: I fucked up. I know I did. Let me fix this.

Omar: I love you. Just answer the phone.

Delivered.

Not read.

Then—

His phone rang.

Jaylen.

Omar exhaled, gripping the phone. "Yo—"

"Nigga."

Omar closed his eyes. Jaylen's voice was calm. Too calm.

"Where the fuck are you?"

Omar hesitated. "I—"

"You at that bitch house?"

Silence.

Omar rubbed a hand over his beard, jaw clenched.

Jaylen let out a short, humorless laugh. "Yeah. That's what the fuck I thought."

"I ain't ask for this shit," Omar muttered.

Jaylen scoffed. "You ain't ask? You sure? 'Cause last time I checked, you made a whole-ass decision."

Omar leaned forward, elbows on his knees. "Jay—"

"Nah. Shut the fuck up. You need to hear this."

Omar's grip tightened.

"You lost Nya, nigga."

Omar's stomach turned.

"She ain't even saying shit. That's how done she is."

Omar said nothing.

Jaylen's voice dropped. "Your name getting dragged in the family chat. Geneva talking shit. Calia talking shit. Even A.O. mad. You really thought you wasn't gonna feel this?"

Omar's chest got tighter.

Jaylen paused, then:

"You sure you don't want me to handle her?"

Omar's breath hitched. "No."

"I know where she live. I could fix this for you."

"Jaylen. I said no."

Jaylen sighed. "Aight. But when she start moving like she got power? Don't say I ain't offer."

Silence.

"Figure out what the fuck you gon' do, O. But don't call me when this shit gets worse."

Click.

Omar stared at the phone.

More regret.

No way to fix it.

His foot tapped against the floor.

Everything was unraveling.

Nya.

His home.

His life.

He stared at his phone.

Jaylen wasn't fucking with him.

Nya wasn't responding.

The family was already talking.

The only one left?

A.O.

He hit call.

Ring.

Ring.

Then—

Click.

"What."

Omar's chest sank.
No warmth. No welcome.

"You heard?"

A.O. let out a low, humorless breath. "Nigga. Everybody heard."

Omar closed his eyes. "Look, man, I need—"

"You need to handle your shit."

"A.O.—"

"Nah. You grown. You made that choice. What the fuck you calling me for?"

"Because I ain't got nobody else."

Long silence.

Then:

"You at her house?"

Omar's voice was small. "Yeah."

"Pathetic."

Omar flinched. "Nigga—"

"You a disappointment, Omar."

Those words hit harder than everything else.

A.O. didn't speak just to speak. If he said it, he meant it.

Another long silence.

"You want me to help you fix this?" A.O.'s voice was low, calm, but sharp.

Omar swallowed hard. "Yeah."

A.O. smirked. "Nah. I'm good."

"A.O., come on, man—"

"You think I got time for this bullshit? I'm handling real business, nigga. You out here moving like a hoe."

"I ain't—"

Click.

Call ended.

Omar stared at the phone.
Nobody was coming to save him.

He was on his own.

He turned slowly, eyes landing on Sienna, still sprawled across the bed, watching him like she had all the time in the world.

She stretched, yawned. "Rough call?"

"Stay outta my business," he muttered.

Sienna smirked. "Baby, I am your business now."

Omar stood. "I gotta go."

"Where?"

Omar froze.

She was right.

He had nowhere to go.
Nya had probably locked him out.
A.O. was done.

Jaylen too.

Omar rubbed his face, sinking back onto the edge of the bed.

Sienna sat up, watching him. "You ain't got nowhere to be, O."

He didn't answer.

"You might as well just stay."

"I ain't staying here."

"Then go."

Omar didn't move.

"Exactly."

She leaned forward, her voice a whisper. "Come on, O. Stop fighting it. You here. Might as well get comfortable."

Omar's chest tightened.

And he hated that she was right.

He should've left.

Should've walked out.
Should've done anything else.

But he didn't.

He sat back down.

And that?

That was the real mistake.

Sienna stretched out beside him, slow, easy.

"See?" she whispered. "Ain't so bad, right?"

Omar didn't respond.

Because deep down?

She was right.

With Nya, he had to prove himself.
Earn it.
Justify his place.

With Sienna?
No expectations.
No pressure.

Just escape.

She crawled toward him, her fingers grazing his thigh.

"You thinking too much," she whispered.

Then she slid down.

And everything else disappeared.

◆ ◆ ◆

The knock was loud.

Too loud.

Omar blinked awake, disoriented, his body heavy from sleep.

Sienna stirred beside him, stretching with a soft sigh. "What time is it?"

Omar grabbed his phone, his stomach dropping instantly.

Missed calls.
Texts.

And one name that made his chest tighten—

Jaylen: Open the fucking door.

Omar sat up fast.

Then—

Boom.

The door flew open.

Before he could even process what the fuck was happening, Jaylen stormed in, his face dark, body moving like a loaded gun.

Right behind him?

Apollo.

And then?

A.O.

Omar's stomach dropped.

Sienna pulled the sheets up, wide-eyed. "What the fuck?!"

A.O. didn't even look at her. Didn't say shit.

Jaylen was already at the bed, grabbing Omar by the shirt and yanking him up.

"Get the fuck up."

Omar jerked away. "Nigga, chill—"

Boom.

Jaylen's fist cracked across his jaw, sending him stumbling back.

Before he could recover, Apollo was there, grabbing him by the arm and dragging him toward the door.

Sienna screamed, scrambling out of bed. "Y'all got me fucked up! What the hell is this?!"

A.O. finally spoke, voice low, calm, and dangerous.

"Shut the fuck up."

Sienna froze.

Jaylen stepped back up, grabbing Omar by the collar again, getting right in his face.

"You done playing, nigga?"

Omar's breath was ragged, jaw throbbing, his mind still catching up.

Jaylen smirked, but it wasn't playful.

"Good. Now let's go."

They dragged him out the house.

No shirt. No shoes. Just shame.

The Escalade waited out front, engine already running like they'd planned this hours ago.

Omar got tossed into the backseat like luggage. The doors shut fast behind him.

Jaylen climbed into the passenger seat, jaw still tight.

Apollo was behind the wheel, silent, unreadable, eyes forward.

A.O. slid in beside Omar, calm. Too calm.

Nobody said shit.

The engine hummed. The silence stretched.

Omar's heart pounded harder with every mile.

Wherever they were going, it wasn't to talk.

The SUV rolled through side streets and turned down a quiet industrial stretch. No traffic. No noise.

Eventually, it slowed to a stop in a near-empty lot behind what used to be an old strip club. Now just concrete, shadows, and streetlight.

Apollo put it in park.

Nobody moved.

Then—

"Get out," A.O. said.

Omar hesitated.

Jaylen didn't even look back. "Nigga, don't make me drag you twice."

Omar exhaled hard and stepped out.

A.O. followed.

The door shut behind them.

The others stayed in the SUV, letting the streetlamps do the talking.

Omar turned toward his brother-in-law, chest still tight. "You ain't have to do all that."

A.O. tilted his head. "Didn't I?"

Omar clenched his jaw. "I ain't a fuckin' kid."

A.O. smirked, unbothered. "Then stop acting like one."

Omar let out a sharp breath, pacing a few feet before turning back. "You don't know what the fuck I'm dealing with, A.O."

"I don't?" A.O. exhaled, tone cool. "Nigga, I been dealin' with you fucking up my money, my rep, your weak-ass street work, for years."

Omar's jaw flexed.

"But now?" A.O. stepped closer. "Now you fucking

with my family."

His voice got lower, dead serious.

"My wife's sister. You think I wanna hear about your little soap opera while I'm tryna get some pussy at night?"

Omar swallowed hard.

A.O. didn't stop.

"You know how many fuck-ups I cleaned up behind you? How many times I told Nya you were 'just focused on music'? Gave her some bullshit reason to stay down with you?"

Another step closer.

"But this?" He pointed toward the direction of Sienna's house. "This some clown shit."

Omar dropped his gaze, jaw clenched so tight it ached.

A.O. took a breath, tone cold now. "You think you still got control. But let me tell you somethin', O…"

His voice cut like glass.

"You lost already."

Omar's breath hitched.

"You lost your home."

Another step.

"You lost your wife."

"And if you keep playin' stupid?" A.O.'s tone dipped even lower. "You gon' lose everything else."

Omar stared at the ground.

Shame. Heat. Guilt. All of it pressing into his skin like weight.

"What you want me to do?" he finally asked, voice hoarse.

A.O. exhaled through his nose. "Fix it."

Then he turned without another word, walking back toward the SUV.

Omar just stood there, jaw tight, chest caved in.

Because A.O. was right.

He had already lost.

Now?

He just had to figure out if anything was still worth saving.

9

The barbershop buzzed low with clippers and quiet tension, TBE's unofficial war room, tucked behind faded posters and fresh fades.

This was where real business got handled.

No cameras. No wires. Just mirrors, clippers, and low voices behind locked doors.

King had more product this time, double.

The deal was locked.
The money was moving.

And A.O.?

Maybe it was pity. Maybe strategy. Either way, he handed Omar six keys without a word.

No discussion.
No negotiation.

Just dropped the package in front of him like a test.

Omar didn't flinch.

Didn't ask no questions.

He knew what it was.

This wasn't about the weight.
It was about whether he was still worth the risk.

Still valuable.
Still useful.

He wasn't in a position to refuse.

And A.O. didn't expect him to.

Omar took the bricks, jaw tight, heart thudding behind his silence.

He had a job now.
Something to focus on.

Something to keep his hands busy and his mind off the rest of his life collapsing in slow motion.

Even if, deep down, he knew six bricks couldn't patch a crumbling life.

A.O. didn't say anything else, just gave Omar a look that meant we done here.

Omar gave a tight nod, turned, and slipped out the back without another word.

As the shop door clicked shut behind him, A.O. kept moving.

He walked through the back hallway, past the spare chairs and supply sink, and into the real room—the one behind the mirrors and jokes, where decisions held weight.

Jah was already there, waiting.

He sat across from A.O., shoulders squared, his phone face-down on the table.

Between them sat a black duffel bag.

Heavy.

Full.

He already knew what was inside before A.O. even spoke.

A.O.'s voice was calm, but sharp. "You know what happens if this don't hit on time."

Jah nodded, face unreadable. "Yeah."

A.O. just stared at him.
Silent.
Waiting.

Jah exhaled through his nose, rubbing the back of his head. "I got it."

A.O. tapped his fingers against the table. "You sure?"

Jah's jaw flexed. "Nigga, I been handling this."

A.O. nodded toward the bag. "Then handle it."

Jah reached for it, his fingers closing around the straps.

But before he could lift it, A.O.'s voice dropped lower, quiet, deliberate.

"You ever fuck this up, nigga?" He tilted his head slightly. "We don't exist no more."

Jah's pulse ticked.

This wasn't just a bribe.
This wasn't just about keeping the feds off their back.

This was the spine of the whole operation.

The reason A.O. was free.
The reason they all were.

Jah nodded slowly, gripping the bag tighter. "I know."

A.O. leaned back, finally satisfied. "Good."

Jah stood, tucking the bag under his arm.

His expression didn't change.

But inside?

The pressure was mounting.
And one wrong move?

Everything crumbled.

◆ ◆ ◆

The house was full.

Voices echoed from the kitchen, spilled down the hallway, filled every room.

But it wasn't loud in a cheerful way. It was loud in that suffocating way. like the volume was meant to keep Nya from hearing the silence of her own heartbreak.

She sat on the couch, staring blankly at the flickering TV screen, the remote still in her lap. Her body was still, but her mind? Spinning.

Everything she thought she knew had been cracked wide open.

Calia's heels clicked across the hardwood. Back and forth. Back and forth.

"I swear to God, I'm this close to calling my brother and telling him to really handle this nigga."

Geneva, perched on the arm of a nearby chair, arms

folded, didn't even flinch. "Calia. A.O. already did enough. This ain't a street problem."

Calia scoffed. "Like fuck it's not. Omar wanna act like he not tied to a whole empire? Like he can just embarrass my cousin on some regular nigga shit?"

She turned and pointed to Nya. "He disrespected her in public. Ain't no coming back from that."

Alisha, seated quietly next to Nya, rubbed slow, soothing circles on her back. "Nya, baby, say something."

But Nya couldn't.

Couldn't form the words. Couldn't find the breath. Couldn't do anything but sit there and feel the ache hollowing her chest.

Charlotte shifted in the corner, legs crossed, arms hugging her midsection. "Niggas are stupid."

Geneva nodded slowly. "Stupid and selfish."

"Same thing," Charlotte muttered.

Nya blinked hard, but the tears still welled up.

She hadn't even gotten to mourn what she lost, because she was still trying to understand what the fuck had happened. How someone who said he loved her could turn around and tear their entire life apart.

Deonte's girl, A, leaned forward, voice low and unreadable. "What you wanna do, Nya?"

All eyes turned to her.

Nya swallowed, her throat burning. "I don't know."

Alisha squeezed her hand. "That's okay. You don't gotta know right now."

Geneva shifted slightly, her tone casual, but there was an edge beneath it. "If you decide you wanna talk to someone... I got a number."

Nya turned toward her, brow furrowed. "What kind of someone?"

Geneva hesitated just long enough.

Then: "A lawyer."

The air shifted.

Nya's eyes widened, but it was Calia who caught on first.

Geneva didn't blink, didn't clarify. Just reached into her purse and pulled out a card, sliding it onto the coffee table like it meant nothing.

Like she hadn't just let a whole truth slip out.

Calia raised an eyebrow. "You been looking into divorce lawyers?"

Geneva didn't answer right away. Just looked straight ahead, calm. "Everybody needs options."

Nya looked down at the card. Michael A. Renner, Esq.

She didn't pick it up. Didn't touch it.

But she saw it.

And she knew.

Knew Geneva had been watching Jah closer than she let on. Knew maybe she wasn't the only one feeling like the foundation they stood on was starting to crack.

"I just... I don't get it," Nya said, her voice cracking.

Charlotte exhaled, rubbing her temples. "You ain't supposed to. Love don't make sense."

Geneva's eyes softened. "Loving him ain't the same as keeping him."

Calia wasn't trying to hear it. "Tell her that when he's showing up at her job with flowers and guilt."

Alisha, still next to Nya, brushed a tear from her cheek. "You don't gotta do anything right now, Nya. You don't owe nobody shit."

But Calia stepped forward, her tone sharper. "No. She needs to say it."

"Calia—" Geneva warned, but Calia ignored her.

"Nya, look at me," she said, kneeling in front of her.

Nya did, eyes bloodshot, face wet.

"You done, right?"

Nya didn't answer.

Calia's voice dropped. "Tell me you done. Tell me you ain't finna be that girl that gets walked over and still stands at the door waiting."

Nya's chin quivered. "I still love him."

Calia closed her eyes, exhaling hard through her nose.

Silence.

The kind that settles in your bones.

Charlotte got up and walked to the window, arms still crossed. "Love ain't enough, Nya."

Alisha held her tighter.

Geneva stared at the lawyer's card, then at Nya. "You don't have to say you're done. Just say you're not okay. That's enough."

Nya broke again. Her shoulders shook, sobs rising from deep in her chest.

She wasn't okay.

Not even close.

And maybe for the first time, she didn't have to pretend to be.

Calia didn't say anything else. Just stood up, jaw locked, eyes stormy.

Charlotte turned back from the window, glancing toward Geneva. "That lawyer good?"

Geneva nodded slowly. "Real good."

Another silence.

But this time, it wasn't heavy.

It was full of something else.

Possibility.

Nya looked down at the card again.

She still didn't pick it up.

But now?

She was thinking about it.

And somewhere deep inside her, the part of her

that still remembered who she was before Omar, the dancer, the dreamer, the woman who took nobody's shit, that part?

She was starting to stir.

◆ ◆ ◆

Jah sat at his desk, staring at the numbers, stomach in knots.

They added up.

That was the problem.

The office buzzed quietly outside his door, muffled phones ringing, distant footsteps, the low murmur of conversations.

But inside?

It was too quiet.

Boss: Jah, need to see you ASAP. Bring your latest reports.

His chest tightened.

This was bad.

Real bad.

He'd been shifting money around for weeks, trying to cover the holes, keep the machine running, pay off debts before anyone noticed. A wire here. A backdated transaction there. All smoke and mirrors.

But now?

Someone was looking.

His leg bounced under the desk, one hand rubbing hard over his face.

He needed to put the money back.

Fast.

Before this turned into something that couldn't be explained.

Before it turned into something that ended everything.

Jah grabbed his phone, thumb hovering.

He had one call to make.

One last shot to fix it.

If it didn't work?

He wasn't just losing his job.

He was losing everything.

◆ ◆ ◆

Jah adjusted his tie, exhaling slow as he stepped into the office. His pulse wouldn't settle.

He had done this before, walked into rooms and made people believe whatever he needed them to.

But today?

He wasn't sure it would be enough.

His boss sat behind the desk, arms folded, eyes sharp, scanning the reports Jah had laid out.

"Jah," he said, voice even. "These numbers don't make sense."

Jah nodded, keeping it smooth. "I know. I caught the

errors this morning. Looks like some transactions were misallocated, I'll have it cleaned up before end of week."

His boss leaned back in his chair, studying him. "So this was a mistake?"

Jah held his gaze. "Yes."

The silence that followed was long. Heavy.

Jah didn't blink.

Didn't move.

Finally, his boss sighed, tossing the reports on the desk. "You've been here a long time. I'm giving you one chance to make this right."

Jah nodded. "I appreciate that."

His boss pointed. "Fix it. Fast."

Jah stood, buttoning his jacket. "I will."

He walked out like the crisis was over.

Like he still had a shot.

Then—

His phone buzzed.

Unknown Number: Your drop is scheduled. One week. Don't be late.

Jah stared at the screen, pulse pounding.

One week.

To make the wire hit.

To cover the bribe.

To plug a hole that was only getting deeper.

Because if he slipped now?

It was all coming down.

And nobody, not A.O., not his firm, not even God, was going to save him from that.

10

Omar booked the nicest penthouse in Vegas.
Floor-to-ceiling windows.
Marble bathroom.
A bed big enough to make him forget he was sleeping in it alone.

But even with all that?

He couldn't breathe.

Because Nya?
She was gone.

And Sienna?
She was everywhere.

He sat on the edge of the bed, phone in hand, thumb hovering over the screen.

Omar: Baby, please.
Omar: I know I fucked up, but don't shut me out like this.
Omar: Just talk to me. One time.

Delivered.
Never read.

His throat tightened.
His heart?
Fucking aching.

Then—

Buzz. Buzz. Buzz.

Another name.
Another problem.

Sienna: You really tryna act like we ain't got something?
Sienna: I know you feeling this too, O.
Sienna: Come back. Let's finish what we started.

Omar exhaled hard, dragging a hand down his face.

His whole world was crashing.

And the worst part?

He was the one who lit the match.

Omar was fucked up.

Whiskey burned down his throat as he sat on the balcony of his penthouse, the city stretching beneath him like it had all the answers.

But it didn't.
Nothing did.

Because Nya wasn't here.

And no matter how much money he had, no matter how many times he tried to drown the ache in his chest, nothing made it stop.

He glanced at his phone, blurry vision struggling to focus.

Omar: Baby please. Just talk to me.
Omar: You don't gotta forgive me, just let me see you.
Omar: Nya.

Delivered.

Never read.

His jaw tensed.
His pulse pounded.

He wasn't about to sit here and keep begging.
Not tonight.

He stood up too fast, the glass slipping from his hand and shattering against the balcony tile. He didn't even flinch.

Moments later, his car swerved slightly as he pulled up to the house, his house.
Or at least, it used to be.

He stumbled out, the night air slapping him in the face, but it didn't sober him up.
Nothing would.
Not until he saw her.
Not until he fixed this.

He made it to the door, knocking once. Then again.

Then—
Laughter.
From inside.

A man's laugh.

Omar's stomach dropped.

His vision blurred. not from the alcohol, but from pure fucking rage.

The door swung open, and there she was.
Nya.

Looking so damn beautiful, even in her casual sweats, her hair in a loose bun.

But she wasn't alone.

A man stood behind her.
Tall. Smiling. Comfortable.

Omar saw red.

He stumbled forward, pulse thudding like a drum in his ears.

That nigga's voice.
In his house.
With his wife.

Nya's expression changed the second she saw him. "Omar, what the fuck?"

But he wasn't looking at her.
He was looking past her.

At him.

A tall, well-dressed nigga, too relaxed, too confident, too fucking in the way.

Omar's jaw clenched, his hands curling into fists. "Who the fuck is this?" His voice came out low, slurred, dangerous.

The man's face shifted. "Aye. Chill out."

Omar snapped.

"Nigga, you in MY house, with MY wife, telling ME to chill?!"

He lunged.

Nya shoved him back, hard. "Get the fuck out, Omar! You're drunk!"

He stumbled, barely catching himself, but the rage

didn't go anywhere.

"You let this nigga in my house?!" he shouted. "You moved on that fast?!"

Nya's face twisted with disgust. "Nigga, I didn't move on. I moved the fuck on from you."

Omar's chest tightened. But he wasn't done.

He pointed at the dude, eyes bloodshot and wild. "I know niggas like you. You just tryna fuck with her head, huh? Nigga, I'll kill you."

The man stepped forward slightly, calmer than Omar expected. "Ion' know you, bro. And I don't care to. But you need to leave."

Omar gritted his teeth. "Make me."

Nya stepped between them, fury radiating off her. "Enough!" she shouted, pointing toward the door. "Get the fuck out, Omar! I mean it!"

He ignored her. His eyes were locked on the man.

"You hear me, nigga?!" Omar's voice cracked, rage, heartbreak, liquor all boiling over. "You think you gonna take my spot? Think you gonna lay up in my house? Fuck my wife?!"

That was it.

Nya saw red.

She grabbed the front of his jacket, yanked him forward, and shoved him straight back toward the porch.

"Get. The. Fuck. Out!"

Omar staggered.

Then—
The door slammed.
Locked.

Silence.

He stood there, breathing hard, fists shaking.

His whole world was spinning.
His whole fucking life, in flames.

And now?
He was outside.
Cold.
Alone.

And drunk as hell.

Omar didn't know how long he stood there.

Could've been minutes.
Could've been an hour.
But he wasn't leaving.
Not like this.

He pounded on the door again, his voice rough. "Nya! Open the door! We ain't done!"

Silence.

Omar's throat burned, his eyes wild, his chest tight.

Then—

Headlights.

A car pulled up, slow, rolling to a stop right in front of him.

The driver's side door opened.

Jaylen.

He stepped out, calm as ever.

Didn't say shit.

Didn't react.

Just stood there, looking at him.

Omar clenched his jaw. "Mind your business, nigga."

Jaylen smirked. "Oh, I am."

Silence stretched.

Then, Jaylen sighed, shaking his head. "Look at you, O. This what you on now? Standing in the cold outside your wife's house like a pathetic-ass nigga?"

Omar's stomach twisted.

But Jaylen wasn't done.

"She don't want you, bro. You lost."

Omar flinched.

Jaylen leaned against the car, crossing his arms. "You done embarrassing yourself, or you wanna keep the show going?"

Omar just stood there.

He had nothing left to say.

Nothing left to do.

Jaylen nodded toward the car. "Let's go."

Jaylen didn't say shit as he drove.
Didn't look at him.
Didn't even try to make a joke.
Just let the silence speak for itself.

Omar stared out the window, his reflection staring back at him.
This was it.
This was rock bottom.

And he had nobody to blame but himself.

Later, Omar sat on the edge of the bed, vision swimming, the half-empty bottle of whiskey on the nightstand tilting in and out of focus.

His head pounded.
His chest ached.

Everything felt fucking numb.

Jaylen sat across from him, arms crossed, watching him with thinly veiled disgust.

"You really on this shit, huh?"

Omar didn't answer.
Didn't have the energy to.

Jaylen exhaled sharply, rubbing a hand down his face. "Nigga, you embarrassing."

Omar let out a dry, humorless laugh. "You said that already."

Jaylen's jaw tightened. "And clearly, you ain't hear me the first time."

Silence stretched between them.

Then Jaylen stood, grabbing his keys. "I'm out."

Omar barely blinked. "You gonna tuck me in first?"

Jaylen stared at him, expression unreadable.

Then—

"You're a lost nigga."

He turned and walked out, not bothering to slam the door.

The sound of it clicking shut behind him was softer than it should have been.

Omar stared at the floor, his hands shaking.

Slumped back in the chair, phone in hand, whiskey burning in his throat.

His mind was clouded.
Drowning.

Nya was gone.
Jaylen had walked out.

Nobody was coming to save him.

So he did what he knew he shouldn't.
What he told himself he wasn't gonna do.

He hit call.

One ring.

Two.

Then—

Sienna's voice, smooth, knowing.
"I was wondering when you'd call me, baby."

Omar closed his eyes, exhaling slow. "Sienna."

She hummed. "You need me?"

He swallowed, chest tight.
But yeah.

Yeah, he did.

"I'm sending a truck. Be ready."

She laughed, low, sweet. "I already am."

Click.

Omar tossed the phone on the table, staring at the ceiling.

He had made his choice.
And soon?

She'd be on her way.

He didn't know how long he sat there, letting the weight of his life press into his chest.

But when the knock came at the door, he already knew who it was.

He exhaled slowly, rubbing a hand over his face before standing.

His legs felt heavy, sluggish from the liquor, from exhaustion, from everything.

He didn't even hesitate before unlocking the door.

And there she was.

Sienna.

Draped in a sleek, form-fitting black dress, her long hair cascading over her shoulder, her lips curved in a smirk that said everything.

She stepped inside, eyes scanning the penthouse, unimpressed, but approving.

"Nice," she murmured, kicking off her heels as she set a bottle of D'USSÉ on the bar.

Omar didn't respond.

Didn't move.

He just stood there, watching her.

Sienna turned to face him, tilting her head. "You look like you need to relax, baby."

Omar let out a humorless chuckle. "That right?"

She nodded slowly, stepping closer, fingers trailing down his chest.

"I brought something to help with that."

Her hands moved to his shoulders, slowly sliding down his arms, her touch light but deliberate.

Omar didn't stop her.

Didn't push her away.

Because for the first time in days?

He didn't want to think.

Didn't want to feel.

Didn't want to hurt.

Sienna smirked, poured two glasses, handed him

one.

He took it, watching her through the rim as he swallowed the burn.

She sipped hers, then stepped back into him, lips grazing his jaw.

"You gonna let me take care of you or what?"

Omar didn't answer.

Just finished his drink.
Set the glass down beside hers.
Gripped the back of her neck.
Pulled her in.

And just like that.
He let himself fall.

They were tangled in sheets when the phone buzzed.

Then again.
And again.

Sienna stirred beside him, groaning. "Baby, turn that shit off."

Omar ignored her, reaching for his phone, squinting at the screen.

67 new messages.
23 missed calls.

His pulse kicked up.

First text?

Jaylen: You a dumbass nigga.

Omar's brows furrowed.

Then—
Calia: Omar. Please tell me this picture is fake.

Omar sat up fast, head spinning.

Then he saw it.

A blog post.
A photo.

Him and Sienna.

Outside the Conrad.

His arm around her waist.

Her lips close to his ear.

Headline:
Platinum Rapper Omar Miller Moves On Quick With Mystery Woman.

His breath hitched.

His grip tightened around the phone.

Sienna yawned, stretching beside him, completely oblivious.

Calia: Nya blocked you, stop calling her private.

Omar's stomach dropped.

It was done.
It was public.

And this time?

There was no coming back.

11

The studio was quiet.

Too quiet.

Omar sat in the booth, slumped in the chair, eyes heavy from liquor, body weighed down by exhaustion and regret.

The bass from the track thumped low, filling the space, but it didn't drown out the thoughts clawing at his mind.

Everything was falling apart.

Nya.
The family.
The six keys sitting in the duffel beside him.

He had been putting off moving them, slipping too

deep into his own bullshit.

And somebody noticed.

The first sign?

The door.

It creaked open.

Not loud, but enough.

Omar's brows furrowed. He turned slightly, glancing toward the entrance, expecting Jaylen, maybe a producer, somebody familiar.

But when the lights cut out?

His heart stopped.

Pitch black.

Silence.

Then, movement.

Fast. Quiet. Too fucking quiet.

Omar shot up from the chair, his pulse hammering,

his breath sharp.

Then—

A gun pressed against his temple.

Cold.

Steady.

A voice, low, controlled, almost amused.

"Run that shit."

Omar froze.

Another voice, rougher, hyped.

"Now, nigga."

His throat went dry. His hands curled into fists at his sides.

He could barely see, but he felt them.

Two, maybe three of them. Surrounding him.

Somebody flicked on a flashlight, the beam bouncing off the gun barrel.

Omar couldn't even breathe.

Then—

CRACK.

A gun smashed across his face. Hard.

Pain exploded through his skull as he hit the ground, his ears ringing.

A boot pressed down on his chest, hard.

"We ain't playing, nigga. Where the fuck is it?"

Omar coughed, blood pooling in his mouth. His lip was split, his head spinning.

The duffel bag.

They already knew where it was.

This wasn't random.

This was a setup.

The beam of the flashlight cut through the dark, landing on the bag beside the couch.

Omar barely had time to react before one of them snatched it up, unzipping it.

The sound of plastic rustling was loud as fuck.

One of them let out a low whistle. "Damn. Jackpot."

Omar's stomach turned.

This wasn't just money.

This wasn't just some weed or some cash.

This was A.O.'s work.

And it was gone.

He tried to push up, tried to reach for something, anything—

BOOM.

Another hit.

This time, the gun connected with the side of his skull, sending him crashing back down.

His vision blurred.

His breath came in ragged gasps.

Then—

The click of the safety being turned off.

The barrel pressed against his forehead.

And for the first time in his life?

Omar felt it.

Real fear.

Real fucking terror.

He tried to swallow, but his mouth was full of blood.

"Please—"

His voice cracked.

The gunman let out a slow chuckle.

"Please? Nigga, I thought you was tougher than that."

Omar's heart pounded so loud he couldn't hear

anything else.

"Yo, let's just pop this nigga."

The voice was younger, eager.

"Nah, he got a name. Might be useful later."

"So what? You wanna let him slide?"

A beat of silence.

Then—

"Let him live. But let him remember."

The weight on his chest lifted.

The gun disappeared from his forehead.

Then—

A boot swung back.

CRACK.

Everything went black.

◆ ◆ ◆

The beeping was the first thing he heard.

Sharp. Repetitive.

A monitor.

Hospital.

Omar blinked, his vision blurry, his head throbbing.

His mouth was dry. His body felt heavy.

For a second, he didn't remember what happened.

Then, the flashbacks hit.

The gun pressed to his forehead.
The pain exploding in his skull.
The voices laughing as they took everything.

His stomach clenched.

He tried to move, but a sharp pain shot through his ribs, forcing him to groan.

The sound must've alerted someone, because the door swung open.

A familiar face stepped inside.

His manager.

A short, sharp-looking man in a designer suit, his expression tight with frustration.

"You awake," he said, crossing his arms. "Finally."

Omar's throat was raw, his voice hoarse. "How long?"

The manager checked his watch. "A day and a half."

Omar exhaled slowly, his mind still foggy.

Then, the manager pulled out his phone and scrolled. "We already handled the press. Told 'em you got jumped in a robbery, left out the details that could actually ruin you."

Omar's chest tightened.

Because even though they could control the media, they couldn't control the family.

As if reading his mind, his manager sighed. "But your people? They know."

Omar's jaw locked.

The manager stuffed his phone back into his pocket, shaking his head. "You're lucky you're still breathing."

Then, another voice from the doorway.

"Not for long."

Omar froze.

Because he knew exactly who that was.

A.O. stepped inside.

Jaylen right behind him.

And the look in their eyes?

Made the hospital bed feel like a death sentence.
The room felt smaller the second A.O. stepped inside.

The steady beeping of the heart monitor seemed too loud, the air too thick.

Jaylen shut the door behind them, leaning against it,

arms crossed, face unreadable.

But A.O.?

He didn't rush.

Didn't say shit.

Just stood at the foot of the hospital bed, watching.

Omar's pulse kicked up.

Not from fear.

Not from pain.

But from the weight of what was about to happen.

A.O. finally spoke, his voice low, even.

"Where's my shit?"

Omar swallowed, his throat dry.

He already knew there was no right answer.

Still, he tried.

"I got set up." His voice came out hoarse, weak. "I

ain't see it coming."

A.O. let out a slow breath, shaking his head. "Didn't ask all that."

Omar's jaw tightened.

A.O. tilted his head slightly, his expression still unreadable.

"You lost six keys." His tone never changed, like he was stating a fact.

Because he was.

Omar didn't speak.

Didn't blink.

Didn't breathe.

A.O. took another step closer, looking down at him.

"You know what that means?"

Omar's chest ached.

That wasn't just product.
That wasn't just money.

That was A.O.'s empire.

That was a line you didn't cross and survive.

A.O. sighed, rubbing his jaw before finally locking eyes with him.

"You got a week."

Omar's breath hitched. "A week for what?"

A.O. exhaled slow, almost like he pitied him.

"To pay me back."

Omar's stomach dropped.

Jaylen, still leaning against the door, let out a humorless chuckle.

A.O. smirked slightly, but it wasn't friendly.

"You don't come up with my money in seven days?" He shrugged. "Then you not my problem no more."

Omar felt the blood drain from his face.

Because he knew exactly what that meant.

This wasn't a threat.
This was a countdown.

A.O. turned toward the door, already done with him.

"Seven days." His voice was calm. Final.

Then, just like that, he walked out.

Jaylen lingered a second longer, shaking his head before muttering, "I'll miss you, nigga."

Then he was gone too.

The door clicked shut.

And Omar?

Omar was left staring at the ceiling.

Because in one week?

He had to come up with a miracle.

Or die trying.

12

J ay sat in his office, staring at the black duffel bag on the floor beside his desk.

It felt heavier than it should.

Not just in weight.

But in what it meant.

The bribe money.

A.O.'s money.

Money that was supposed to keep the feds in check.

Money that, if it wasn't delivered on time, could fuck up everything.

Jah ran a hand down his face, exhaling slow, trying

to steady his thoughts.

He had no choice.

His firm was breathing down his neck.

The numbers weren't balancing. His boss was already watching him.

If he didn't fix this now, he wouldn't just lose his job, he'd be exposed.

He convinced himself it was temporary.

A short-term move.

He'd pull from the bribe, cover his tracks at work, and replace it before anyone noticed.

The feds weren't expecting the drop for another week.

Seven days.

He could figure something out by then.

He had to.

His leg bounced under the desk, fingers tapping

against the armrest of his chair.

Then—

He reached down, grabbed the bag, and made his decision.

◆ ◆ ◆

Deonte moved carefully.

Brandon wasn't stupid.

If he came too direct, too forceful, the nigga would smell the setup before he even finished his sentence.

So instead?

He played it cool.

Casual.

Like this wasn't the most dangerous conversation he'd ever had.

Brandon was posted up outside the club, smoking, watching the street, his usual post.

Deonte walked up slow, hands in his pockets,

nodding in greeting.

"What's good, B?"

Brandon exhaled, looking him over. "What you want, D?"

Deonte smirked slightly. Straight to it, huh?

"Just a conversation," he said, leaning against the wall beside him. "I know you been hearing shit."

Brandon stayed silent, taking another drag of his blunt.

Deonte continued, keeping his voice low.

"Word is, niggas want war with A.O.," he muttered. "Dru already down. Shit's moving, B."

Brandon didn't react, but Deonte saw the way his jaw tightened slightly.

He was listening.

Deonte exhaled, shaking his head. "A.O. been on top too long. Niggas want blood." He turned slightly, studying Brandon. "You on the right side of this?"

Brandon finally looked at him. Deadpan.

Then, he laughed.

Not a full laugh.

A short, humorless chuckle.

"You serious, nigga?"

Deonte shrugged. "I'm saying—"

Brandon stepped in closer, cutting him off.

"Get the fuck out my face."

Deonte's smirk dropped. "Nigga—"

"You think I don't know what this is?" Brandon's voice was low, dangerous.

"I know who I stand with."

Deonte held his ground, but his pulse ticked.

Brandon exhaled slowly, shaking his head.

"You fucked up comin' to me with this."

Then, he turned and walked inside, leaving Deonte standing there.

Brandon wasn't the type to hesitate.

As soon as he left Deonte, he called Jaylen.

Jaylen answered on the second ring.

"Talk to me."

Brandon's voice was calm, but serious.

"Deonte just came to me talking reckless."

Silence.

Then—

Jaylen sighed, deep and slow.

"Niggas never learn."

Brandon nodded. "He said another gang want war with A.O. Dru already down."

Jaylen didn't speak for a moment.

Then, his voice dropped lower.

"Meet me at the barbershop. Now."

Click.

Jaylen pulled up to the barbershop, stepping inside without hesitation.

A.O. was getting a lineup, eyes closed, relaxed.

But the second Jaylen stepped up, A.O. knew.

He exhaled slowly, eyes still closed.

"Talk."

Jaylen didn't waste time.

"Deonte's moving funny."

A.O. opened his eyes. Sharp. Focused.

Jaylen continued.

"He came up to Brandon. Talking war. Talking about niggas want you out."

A.O. blinked once.

Then, calmly, he turned to the barber.

"We done."

The barber backed up immediately.

A.O. stood, brushing off his shoulders before locking eyes with Jaylen.

"Get everybody in the room."

His voice was quiet.

Deadly.

"Now."

A.O. wasn't going to waste time chasing Deonte.

That nigga wasn't stupid.

He wasn't about to pull up somewhere alone, wasn't about to walk into a setup like a rookie.

But Dru?

Dru was reckless.

Dru was loud.

And more than anything?

Dru had it coming.

Not just for being a disloyal nigga.

But for putting his hands on Charlotte.

A.O. sat in the private backroom of the barbershop, his expression unreadable as he looked at Jaylen.

Jaylen didn't need instructions.

Didn't need explanations.

He just needed a green light.

And A.O. gave it with one look.

Jaylen cracked his knuckles, nodding once. "Bet."
Dru had a routine.

He didn't live with Charlotte full-time, not that she wanted him to.

Most nights, he was either posted up at the club, fucking around with randoms, or gambling.

Tonight?

He was at his usual spot, a private backroom in an underground casino, sipping a drink, laughing like he didn't have a single problem in the world.

He had no idea.

Jaylen walked in smooth, calm, unbothered.

Dru barely looked up at first.

Then, he did a double take. Frowned slightly.

"What's good, Jay? You ain't the type to come through here."

Jaylen sat down across from him, leaning back, expression unreadable.

"Nah. But you the type to switch sides, huh?"

Dru's smirk faltered. "The fuck that mean?"

Jaylen picked up a card from the table, flipping it between his fingers.

"It means you put your money on the wrong nigga."

Dru's jaw tightened.

Jaylen smirked slightly, tilting his head. "What? You thought niggas wasn't gonna find out?"

Dru exhaled through his nose. "Man, listen—"

Jaylen cut him off, his voice low, smooth.

"Nah. You listen."

He set the card down, folding his hands.

"This?" He gestured between them. "Ain't even about business no more."

Dru frowned. "Then what the fuck is it about?"

Jaylen's smirk disappeared.

"It's about Charlotte."

Dru's face twitched.

Jaylen nodded slowly, watching him.

"You thought niggas ain't know? Thought nobody was paying attention?"

Dru scoffed, shaking his head. "Man, that's between me and my wife—"

BOOM.

Jaylen moved before Dru could even register it.

The first shot hit him square in the chest, knocking him back.

Dru gasped, eyes wide, hands gripping his torso, blood spreading fast.

Jaylen stood, calm, unshaken.

"You ain't got no wife, nigga."

Dru tried to speak.

Tried to move.

BOOM.

The second shot hit his head.

The table shook.

The cards scattered.

Jaylen tucked his gun back, exhaling slow before turning toward the door.

He didn't look back.

Didn't need to.

The message was sent.

Deonte would get it loud and clear.

And if he didn't?

He'd be next.

13

The hotel room was dim.

Silent.

Except for the low hum of the TV.

Omar sat on the edge of the bed, a bottle of whiskey beside him, phone in one hand, remote in the other.

He wasn't watching.

Just flipping through channels, mind spiraling.

Then—

BREAKING NEWS.

His thumb froze.

The headline lit up the screen:

"Famous NBA Player Andrew 'Dru' Carter Found Shot to Death in Underground Casino."

Omar's heart pounded.

The screen cut to a shaky video, cops swarming, yellow tape flapping, reporters speaking in hushed, urgent tones.

His stomach turned.

Dru.

Gone.

And he already knew who did it.

His grip on the phone tightened.

He had five days.

Five days to pull together half a million.

Or he was next.

Pulse thundering, Omar hit call.

Jaylen picked up on the second ring, voice light.

"What's up, superstar? You finally paying attention?"

Omar exhaled hard, rubbing his temple. "Nigga, what the fuck is going on?"

Jaylen chuckled. "You tell me. You the one moving slow."

Omar's jaw clenched. "A.O. said half a mil. No less."

Jaylen hummed. "And you got five days. Better hurry up, nigga. Before you make the news next."

Click.

Line dead.

Omar stared at his phone, his whole body tense.

He was running out of time.

And running out of options.

There was only one move left.

Omar sat at the desk in his hotel suite, laptop open, fingers flying across the keys.

His pulse roared in his ears.

He had money.

Millions.

Or at least... he was supposed to.

The plan was simple, pull what he needed, fix this shit, figure the rest out later.

But the second he logged into his account—

His breath caught.

The balance was off.

Way off.

Way lower than it should've been.

He blinked. Refreshed the page.

Still wrong.

Hands curling into fists, he scrolled through the transactions.

And then he saw it.

Large sums.

Transferred.

Moved.

All into an account under a name that made his blood run cold.

Nya.

His vision blurred.

She took the money.

She got to it first.

A cold sweat broke over his skin. His breath grew shallow.

He had nothing now.

No backup.

No plan.

No way out.

◆ ◆ ◆

The streetlights blurred past him as he sped toward Nya's house, his heart pounding against his ribs.

She took everything.

She wasn't just ignoring him.

She wasn't just blocking him.

She was ending him.

And he wasn't about to just sit back and let it happen.

The second he pulled up to the house, he barely put the car in park before jumping out, slamming the door shut.

But the moment he took a step toward the front door, he stopped cold.

Because he wasn't alone.

A.O. leaned against the porch railing, arms crossed, watching him like he had been expecting this.

Jaylen stood next to him, smirking.

Apollo was off to the side, silent, unreadable.

And Brandon?

Brandon was just waiting.

Like if Omar so much as twitched wrong, he was ready to make him regret it.

Omar's breath hitched. His chest tightened.

This wasn't just a pull up and argue with Nya situation.

This was a set up.

Jaylen was the first to speak, amusement dripping from his tone.

"Damn, O. You really thought this was gonna go different, huh?"

Omar clenched his jaw. "Where's Nya?"

Jaylen chuckled, shaking his head.

"Oh, she left. She ain't got time for this dumb-ass nigga shit."

Omar took a step forward, but Apollo moved.

Didn't say shit. Didn't threaten.

Just shifted enough to make Omar freeze.

Jaylen pulled something from his jacket, a stack of papers.

He walked over, took his time unfolding them, then held them out.

"You looking for her? Here you go."

Omar frowned, looking down.

His stomach dropped.

Divorce papers.

His name.

Nya's name.

It was all there.

Legit. Signed. Done.

Omar's vision blurred.

Jaylen's voice cut through it, smug and slow.

"And that nigga you was ready to fight the other night? That wasn't her new man."

Omar's jaw tightened.

Jaylen grinned. "That was her lawyer, dumbass."

Omar felt his breath leave his body.

Like the ground just split open beneath him.

He had been losing Nya.

But now?

He had lost her for good.

A.O. exhaled slow, stepping off the porch, walking right past him, not even sparing him a glance.

"Get outta here, Omar. You losing it."

Apollo followed.

Then Brandon.

Jaylen lingered just a second longer, watching him.

Then he shook his head, smirked, and clapped him on the shoulder.

"Tough break, nigga."

Then he was gone too.

Omar was left standing in the dark, holding the last piece of his marriage in his hands.   \

Omar stood in the driveway, the divorce papers crumpled in his fist.

The house, the one he bought for Nya, the one they built a family in, stood just a few feet away.

But it might as well have been a thousand miles.

Because he wasn't walking through that door ever again.

His chest tightened.
His breath came in shallow, uneven pulls.

The cold night air clung to his skin, but it wasn't enough to cool the fire burning in his veins.

Not anger.
Not rage.

Loss.

This was it.

The end.

He backed away slowly, legs unsteady.

The papers slipped from his hand and fluttered to the pavement.

They hit like nothing.
But they meant everything.

His heart pounded, too hard, too fast.

He reached for the car door, gripping it like an anchor just to stay upright.

Then, before he could stop it—
his whole body gave out.

His forehead dropped against the roof of the car, arms trembling, breath ragged.

His vision blurred.
His throat burned.
His chest caved.

He had been running.
Drinking.
Fucking up.

Trying to outrun this moment.

But there was nowhere left to go.

A rough, broken breath slipped from his lips.

Then, his shoulders shook.

And for the first time in his life?

Omar Oakes broke.

14

A.O. sat in the back of the barbershop. The room was dim.

Still.

Thick with tension.

His phone buzzed.

Unknown number.

But he already knew.

He let it ring once.
Twice.

Then answered, voice flat.

"Talk."

A low chuckle slid through the line.

"One dead nigga don't stop a war."

A.O.'s jaw tightened.

Deonte.

Calm.

Like he knew something A.O. didn't.

"Hope y'all keepin' ya heads on a swivel... would hate to catch somebody slippin'."

Then—

Click.

Silence.

A.O. set the phone down slow, fingers drumming the table once... then stopping.

Jaylen, across from him, let out a sharp breath.

"Nigga really think he got a shot at this."

A.O. didn't flinch.

Didn't blink.

Because this wasn't just talk.

Deonte didn't call to flex.

This was a warning.

Which meant?

Shit was already in motion.

It started the next night.

A low-level dealer got clipped outside a gas station.

Execution-style.

Two shots.

Back of the head.

Nothing taken.

No product.

Just a message.

Then—

Two more got robbed, broad daylight.

Stripped.

Tied up.

Left on the corner like trash.

And when the third body dropped?

The whispers started.

Barbershops.

Dice games.

Corners.

A.O.'s name was ringing.

Not in respect.

In question.

Because in this game?

Power had to be proven.

And Deonte?

He was making his play.

The energy in the room was charged.

Brandon sat at the head of the table, arms crossed, his usual calm intensity masking the fire beneath.

Jaylen leaned against the wall, phone in hand, texting back and forth, setting up the next move.

The shooters were already lined up.

They weren't waiting for another hit.

They weren't sitting back.

This was about control.

A.O. wasn't going to just defend his position.

He was going to remind the city who the fuck ran it.

Jaylen finally put his phone down, nodding toward Brandon. "We hitting three spots tonight."

Brandon smirked slightly. "Who first?"

Jaylen cracked his knuckles. "The nigga that shot our dealer at the gas station? He dies first."

Brandon nodded once. "Clean. Fast. No noise."

Jaylen exhaled through his nose, his tone deadly calm.

"Then we let the other two niggas run."

Brandon raised a brow. "You want survivors?"

Jaylen smirked. "Nah. I want messengers."

Brandon sat back, considering, then nodded. "Aight. Let's get it done."

He turned to the shooters, who were already loading up, checking clips, securing masks.

Jaylen's voice dropped lower.

"Make sure the last thing they hear is Deonte's name."

Because by the time the sun came up?

That nigga was gonna know exactly what was coming.

The retaliation was clean.

Precise.

Two dead, one survivor left to spread the message.

By sunrise, the city knew what time it was.

A.O. wasn't folding.

But Deonte?

He wasn't backing down either.

The first hit came fast.

One of A.O.'s stash houses got hit before noon.

Nobody saw it coming.

By the time the lookouts called it in, it was too late.

Product gone.

Two bodies dropped.

The word spread quick.

This wasn't just beef anymore.

This was war.

And the streets?

They were on fire.

Jaylen was mid-conversation with A.O. when his phone buzzed.

He answered, barely getting a word out before a

panicked voice came through the line.

"Niggas hit the 5th Street spot! Took everything!"

Jaylen's blood ran cold.

He barely had time to react before another call came in.

Another hit.

Another loss.

This wasn't just retaliation, this was escalation.

Jaylen met A.O.'s gaze.

A.O. exhaled slowly, his expression unreadable.

Then, finally—

"We end this."

Because if they didn't?

There wouldn't be nothing left to fight for.

Jaylen and Brandon weren't waiting for the next move.

They were taking it.

Before A.O. could even send the order, the two of them were already mobilizing shooters.

No strategy. No patience.

Just pure retaliation.

By midnight, three of Deonte's spots were hit.

Small crews. Low-level niggas.

Easy targets.

But this wasn't about money or territory anymore.

This was about power.

About sending a message.

And Jaylen?

Jaylen was making sure niggas felt it.

"Leave one." Jaylen's voice was too calm. "Tell him who killed ya man's."

Brandon didn't even wait for Jaylen to finish.

He had his own list.

And his own grudge.

When Deonte's crew hit their stash houses, they didn't just take product.

They left bodies.

People Brandon personally put on.

And now?

Now, he was collecting his debt.

"Line 'em up," he said, calm as hell. "Ain't nobody gone be breathing when we done."

◆ ◆ ◆

A.O. was in the middle of another meeting with contractors for the lounge when his phone blew up.

Four missed calls.

His jaw clenched as he answered the fifth.

Jaylen's voice came through, sounding too damn satisfied.

"We handled that shit."

A.O. exhaled slowly.

"How bad?"

Jaylen chuckled. "Bad enough that they ain't walking this one off."

Silence.

A.O. rubbed a hand over his face, stepping away from the men with him. "Y'all niggas moved without me?"

Jaylen's voice didn't change.

"We did what had to be done."

A.O.'s mind was already working through the consequences.

They crossed a line.

And now, somebody had to die.

15

The sky was gray, thick with heavy clouds that sat low over the city.

The church was packed, too packed.

People who had never even fucked with Dru like that were here, all dressed in black, all sitting in stiff wooden pews, whispering behind gloved hands.

It was the type of funeral where grief mixed with politics.

Where some niggas came to mourn.

And others?

Others came just to be seen.

A.O. and his crew walked in together.

Jaylen. Brandon. Apollo.

Heads turned as soon as they stepped inside.

Eyes locked on them, some filled with quiet acknowledgment, others thick with judgment.

Because showing up, made them look guilty.

Not showing up would've looked worse.

A.O. moved down the aisle to the front, where the weight of everything sat the heaviest.

Charlotte was there.

Dru's mother beside her, face carved from stone, holding a lace handkerchief in her lap, her grief too deep to cry in public.

Charlotte was different.

She was shaking.

Dressed in all black, her face turned slightly down, hands gripping the program so tightly it was wrinkled between her fingers.

Her eyes were swollen, lined with exhaustion, but there was no softness in them.

Just quiet fury.

The preacher's voice echoed through the church, soft at first, then growing, filling the space with empty words about legacy, about loss, about God taking Dru home too soon.

A.O. barely listened.

He just sat there, hands folded in his lap, staring at the casket.

Dru's face was gone.

The funeral home had done what they could, but a bullet to the head didn't leave much to work with.

It was closed casket.

A.O. exhaled slowly, pressing his tongue against the inside of his cheek.

Because no matter what words were said in this church?

No matter how much scripture got read, how many people wept?

This wasn't over.

◆ ◆ ◆

The service had just ended.

The crowd poured out of the church, slow-moving, thick with grief, with whispers, with watchful eyes.

It happened too fast.

One second, they were moving toward the cars, their security already in position.

Then—

POP. POP. POP.

Gunfire ripped through the quiet.

A.O. ducked instantly, hand already reaching for his piece.

Jaylen moved fast, shoving Charlotte down behind a car.

Brandon never got the chance.

A single shot caught him in the side, tearing through flesh, sending him stumbling backward.

A.O. barely had time to react before Apollo was already moving, pulling Brandon behind cover.

Jaylen pulled his own gun, eyes scanning for the shooters.

Another round went off.

A window shattered.

People screamed.

More shots.

More chaos.

Then—

Tires squealing, women and children screaming, people running back toward the church doors.

Brandon was bleeding heavy, his teeth clenched as Apollo pressed a hand against the wound.

"Stay the fuck awake, nigga." Apollo's voice stayed low, but his hands? Moved like a medic in a war zone, tight, fast, focused.

Jaylen wiped blood from his sleeve, his breathing sharp.

"They really tried us at a fucking funeral."

A.O. just stood there, expression unreadable.

Brandon let out a rough breath, trying to sit up.

Jaylen pushed him back down. "Nigga, stay still."

Brandon exhaled through his nose, shaking his head. "These niggas want war?"

His jaw clenched, eyes burning.

"We giving 'em hell."

The sirens came fast.

Too fast.

A.O. barely had time to process anything before blue lights flooded the street, flashing against the shattered glass and bodies still bleeding out.

Then—

"GET ON THE GROUND! HANDS IN THE AIR!"

The voice boomed through the chaos.

A.O. turned his head slowly.

Brandon, still clutching his side, looked up, his face twisted in pain and fury.

Jaylen's jaw clenched as he dropped his gun, hands raising just slightly.

He wasn't the type to go down quiet.

The second they grabbed him, he jerked back, chest rising, voice sharp.

"Fuck off me! Them niggas shot at us and we getting flickes! This a setup!"

The cops didn't care.

Didn't say shit.

Just twisted his arm harder, forcing him down onto

the pavement.

Jaylen let out a rough laugh, voice dripping with rage and exhaustion.

"Yeah, aight. Do y'all job then. I'll be out before lunch."

But when the cop leaned down, voice low in his ear?

The words made his stomach drop.

"You ain't going nowhere, nigga. This a fed case."

Brandon's blood was still leaking through his shirt, staining his hands, his jeans, the pavement beneath him.

The EMTs were trying to get to him, but the cops didn't give a fuck.

Didn't care that he was barely sitting upright, his breathing shallow, his face pale.

They just slapped the cuffs on him anyway.

Apollo stood next to him, silent.

Watching.

His fists clenched at his sides, his jaw locked, but he didn't speak.

Didn't fight.

Didn't move.

Because he already knew how this worked.

Brandon let out a ragged breath, body going limp as they lifted him onto the stretcher

"We should've hit them first."

16

They got snatched on a Sunday.

By Monday morning, the news was everywhere, mugshots, rumors, headlines. "RICO Sweep Takes Down Alleged Drug Ring." A.O., Jaylen, and Brandon. Faces plastered across every blog, every feed, every group chat.

They didn't get bail right away.

This wasn't that type of case.

Nah.

This was federal.

So they sat.

Held without bond while the feds laid out their little

PowerPoints, wire taps, surveillance stills, bank records, street chatter.

By Wednesday, the hearing started.

And everybody pulled up.

The courtroom looked like a fashion show and a funeral at the same time, Calia in heels, Geneva in pearls, Alisha in silence. Jah in the back, head down, phone buzzing like a heartbeat. Omar somewhere in the cut with his hoodie pulled low. Ain't nobody say a word.

The prosecutor made it sound like they were the cartel. Called A.O. "the mastermind." Jaylen "an enforcer." Brandon "a key player in a violent enterprise." Said they had resources. Connections. Flight risk. Said if they got out, the whole city would bleed.

The judge listened. Stone-faced. Unbothered.

Then their lawyers took over.

Spoke smooth. Said they were family men. Businessmen. Tied to their communities. That the charges were just allegations. No convictions. That holding them without bond was punishment before proof.

The judge didn't budge.

Not that day.

But he scheduled the next hearing for Friday.

And by then?

The energy had shifted.

They walked in with different posture. Heads high. Shoulders squared. Like somebody knew something. Like something had been worked out behind the scenes.

When the judge came back in, the courtroom damn near stopped breathing.

He cleared his throat, flipped through his papers slow like it wasn't a thousand lives hanging on what he was about to say.

"Bail is granted."

A ripple of sound, gasps, relief, quiet cries.

Then:

"Five million dollars. Each."

And just like that, the breath left the room again.

Not assets. Not property. Not no ten percent games.

Cash.

Clean.

Verified.

The kind of bail meant to keep a man caged.

But something was already moving.

Calls got made. Banks got contacted. Accounts got pulled.

Nobody said who.

Nobody had answers.

But by Monday?

That wire hit.

The system stalled for a second, trying to figure out

if it was real.

By Tuesday morning, the paperwork cleared.

The guards walked them out in fresh clothes, wrists free, chins up.

A.O. stepped into the sun like he never left it.

Jaylen grinned like he knew something the rest of the world didn't.

Brandon limped out slow, shoulder wrapped, eyes low.

The streets buzzed.

Everybody wanted to know who paid it.

But nobody said a word.

And the crew?

They ain't have time to celebrate.

Because now the real work had to start.

The house was quiet.

A.O. leaned back in his chair, one ankle rested over his knee, swirling the dark liquor in his glass, his face unreadable.

Jaylen was posted on the couch, arms stretched along the back, legs wide, but his eyes were locked on Omar like a trigger waiting to be pulled.

Brandon stood off to the side, near the wall, one shoulder slightly leaned, but his body still tense.

Stiff from the healing wound.

Eyes sharp.

At the bar, Calia, Geneva, and Alisha were quiet.

Watching.

Listening.

But staying out the way.

And Nya?

She was perched on the edge of the loveseat, legs

crossed at the ankle, back straight, arms folded.

Her expression gave nothing away, but her energy?

Cold.

She hadn't looked at Omar once since he walked in.

Not even a glance.

The silence dragged.

Then—

A.O. set his glass down with a soft clink.

"Alright, nigga," he said finally, his voice low. "Talk."

Omar leaned forward slightly, elbows on his knees.

"About what?"

A.O. stared at him.

"Don't play dumb. You came up with 15 mil' in less than twenty-four hours. That don't just happen."

Omar's jaw tensed.

Jaylen chuckled, no humor in it. "Nah, for real. You ain't never moved that smart before."

Brandon shook his head, a dry smile pulling at the corner of his mouth. "Nigga went from fumbles to Forbes overnight."

Omar let them talk.

Let the jokes hit the air and settle.

Then he spoke.

Calm. Clear.

"I sold my masters. Took an advance from the label."

Everything froze.

Jaylen sat up straighter.

A.O.'s brow lifted, just slightly. "You did what?"

Omar looked at him dead-on.

"I sold my masters," he repeated. "Took an advance."

Jaylen stared, mouth parting like he didn't believe it.

"Nigga… your whole catalog?"

Omar nodded once.

Jaylen exhaled long and low, shaking his head. "Damn. So they own you now."

Omar didn't respond.

The check he got for it? That money came with chains. Long-term interest. Label control.

It'd take years to buy himself back.

If he ever could.

But what was he supposed to do?

Let A.O. rot behind bars?

Let Jaylen and Brandon sit in a cell while he clutched onto some old hits and ego?

"I did what I had to do," he said, voice firm.

A.O. leaned back again, his hands clasped in front of him now, lips pressed together.

"You ain't even think to come to me first," he said.

Not angry.

Just... disappointed.

Omar swallowed hard. "Would you have let me?"

Across the room, Nya finally looked up.

Just once.
Long enough to meet Omar's eyes.

The house was quiet again.

Most of the crew had left.

Calia had taken the women upstairs.

Jaylen and Brandon were in another room, already plotting.

It was just A.O. and Omar now.

A.O. sat back on the leather couch, slowly rolling his glass of liquor in one hand, the ice clinking softly.

His eyes never left Omar.

Studying him.

Weighing him.

Omar stood tall across from him.

Shoulders squared.

Posture steady.

Not folding.

Not today.

He wasn't the same fuck-up A.O. had been checking these last few months.

And A.O. saw that.

Felt it.

He exhaled, slow and deliberate, then set his glass down on the table with a quiet clink.

Finally, he spoke.

"We even now."

Omar's chest tightened, but he didn't flinch.

He knew exactly what that meant.

No more debts.
No more quiet favors.
No more weight hanging over his head.

"Aight," he said simply.

A.O. let it hang there.
Let the silence stretch a little longer.
Then a small smirk tugged at his lips.

"I should still beat your ass, though."

Omar cracked a dry chuckle. "For what?"

A.O. leaned forward, elbows resting on his knees.
His tone dropped.

"For losing my fucking work."

The smirk faded from Omar's face.
He nodded once, slow.

"Yeah. I deserved that."

A.O. studied him, eyes sharp, unreadable.
Then he nodded too. Just slightly.

"But you showed up."

Pause.

A shift in the air.

The tension didn't break.
It just changed.

A.O. leaned back again, tapping the side of his glass with two fingers.

"Doesn't mean shit yet, though. You still gotta prove yourself."

Omar didn't hesitate.

"How?"

A.O. poured himself another drink.
His face stayed hard as he stared at the amber liquid, letting it swirl once before settling.

"While we were locked up, Deonte hit us."

Omar's jaw clenched.
He already knew some of it.

Had been watching the streets shift, feeling the tension creeping back in.

But hearing it from A.O.?

It hit different.

"He took corners. Hit our runners. Cleaned out two stash houses."

A.O. exhaled through his nose.

"We gotta start over."

Omar nodded once. "We got money problems?"

A.O. took a slow sip.

"We got no fucking money."

Omar exhaled, slow. This was deeper than he thought.

A.O. set the glass down, locking eyes with him now.

"But I got a plan."

Omar straightened. He knew what was coming. Felt it in the air.

A.O. leaned forward, voice steady.

"Me, Jaylen, Brandon, we gotta fall back. Feds watching everything now."

Omar didn't speak. He just listened.

"That means it's on you and Jah."

The words settled between them.

Omar felt the weight of them.
No more safety net.
No more playing the background.

This was his call-up.

A.O. tapped the table once, sharp.

"This your chance, O. You and Jah gotta move like bosses."

Omar met his gaze. "Bet."

A.O. didn't smile. Didn't nod.
Just looked at him for a beat.

Without another word, he grabbed his phone and dialed.

"Tell Jah to come in."

◆ ◆ ◆

A.O. had always believed real power moved in silence.

And even behind federal walls, he moved like a boss.

In the 10 days he was locked up, he made real connections.
Men who didn't just run corners or cities.

Men who moved continents.

Men who didn't blink at war.

Now?
One of them was offering a way back in.

But this wasn't no small-time re-up.
This was high-level, life-changing weight.

Colombian pure.

Sixty keys.
1 month to flip it and pay it back.

And the catch?

They had to go get it themselves.
No middlemen.
No runners.
No safety net.
Just Omar and Jah.

A.O. sat in his home office, fresh out but already rebuilding.
The walls still smelled like new paint, but the energy?
All old power.

Jah stood across from him, arms stiff, hands on his hips, pacing like he needed somewhere else to be.

"You serious?" he asked, voice low but sharp.

A.O. didn't flinch. Just lifted his glass and took a slow sip.
"Dead serious."

Jah exhaled, shaking his head. "That's international weight, nigga. That's fed time if we get caught."

A.O. gave a lazy shrug. "We ain't gettin' caught."

Jah shot a look at Omar, who was leaned against the desk, arms crossed like he'd already made peace with the plan.

Jah's voice cut in again. "And him? You really think he ready for this?"

Omar didn't move, didn't blink. His voice came calm and cool.

"You doubting me, Jah?"

Jah scoffed. "I ain't doubting. I'm asking. You ever moved sixty bricks before?"

Omar's jaw flexed, but his tone stayed smooth. "First time for everything."

Jah looked back at A.O., frustration creeping in. "This the move you wanna make? Right out the gate?"

A.O. leaned forward, eyes steady. "You both handle this right, we not just bouncing back, we running the whole coast."

Silence fell again, heavy as a loaded gun.

Jah let out a breath through his nose. "And if we don't?"

A.O. didn't blink.
Didn't smirk.

Just stared straight through him.

"Then you better pray Colombian niggas don't move like we do."

17

O mar sat across from Nya at the dining room table, elbows resting on the polished wood like he didn't know what to do with his hands. The house was quiet, too quiet. Alya was asleep upstairs. The dishwasher hummed in the background. But in here, in this moment?

It was dead.

Nya didn't speak.

Didn't fidget. Didn't blink.

She just watched him.

Waited.

He took a breath, then another. His fingers laced together like a prayer.

"I fucked up," he said.

Still, nothing from her. Not a twitch. Not even a sigh. Because she already knew. She always did.

Omar looked down at his hands. His voice dropped.

"I lied. About the gang. About the money. About… everything."

The weight of it sat heavy on the table between them.

"And I cheated."

That time, she reacted, barely. A sharp inhale, soft enough to miss unless you were waiting for it.

But he was.

Omar's throat tightened. "I wasn't thinking. I let shit get outta control."

He glanced up. Her eyes were still on him. Cold. Still.

"I was reckless, Nya. And I hurt you."

Finally, she moved. Leaned back slowly, arms folding

across her chest.

"You hurt me?" Her voice was calm, almost conversational. That was how he knew he was in real trouble.

Omar nodded. "Yeah. And I'm sorry."

Her lips pressed together, brow lifting like she couldn't believe how weak that landed.

"You're sorry," she repeated. "That's it?"

"I don't know what else to say."

She laughed, just once. Low and bitter. "You always don't know what to say. Until it's too late."

He rubbed his palms together. "Nya, I—"

"Did she mean anything?"

He froze.

She tilted her head. "The girl. Did she mean anything to you?"

Silence.

And that pause?

That was all the answer she needed.

Nya nodded, slow and steady, then stood. Her chair scraped against the floor, jarring in the quiet.

"You couldn't even lie to make it better," she said, voice flat.

Omar rose fast, heart pounding. "Nya, wait—"

"For what?" she snapped. "So you can tell me more half-truths? Make promises you're not built to keep?"

"I'm done lying. That's why I'm telling you now."

She turned toward the stairs.

"Can we fix this?" he asked, the words catching in his throat.

She stopped. Didn't turn around. Didn't speak.

And when she did, her voice was so soft he almost didn't hear it.

"I don't know."

Then she was gone.

And all Omar could do was stare at the place she'd been, wondering if he'd just lost the only thing that ever really kept him grounded.

Geneva stood by the window, arms crossed tight across her chest. Outside, the streetlights flickered against the quiet, suburban night. Inside, the silence was suffocating.

Jah sat on the edge of the bed behind her, hunched over with his elbows on his knees. His hands were clasped, knuckles white. He'd been trying to figure out how to start for damn near an hour.

He finally let out a slow breath. "I need to tell you something."

Geneva didn't move. Didn't blink. Just kept her eyes on the street like whatever was out there was more important than him.

Jah continued anyway. "I've been gambling."

Nothing.

"A long time. More than you know."

Her shoulders tensed, but still, she didn't turn.

"I owe money. Over a hundred grand."

That hit. Her spine stiffened.

Jah closed his eyes for a moment, pushing the next words out like they tasted foul. "And I covered it using money that wasn't mine."

Now she turned.

Slow. Controlled.

"What do you mean?"

Jah looked up at her. His eyes were bloodshot. Tired. Defeated.

"I embezzled," he said. "From work."

Geneva stared at him like she didn't recognize who he was. Her lips parted, but no words came out. She took a step closer. Her voice cracked when she finally spoke.

"You stole from the hedge fund?"

Jah nodded once.

She pressed a hand to her chest, like she needed to feel her own heartbeat to know this was real. "How long?"

Jah hesitated. "Almost a year."

Geneva's jaw clenched. She turned away again, pacing in a tight circle before stopping at the dresser.

"And A.O.?" she asked, her voice tight. "This ties back to him, doesn't it?"

Jah swallowed hard. "The feds came to me first. I was supposed to deliver a bribe to keep them off A.O.'s back."

Her head snapped toward him. "And?"

"I didn't," he said quietly. "I used the money to pay off part of my debt."

Geneva took a sharp breath, staggering slightly like the truth had physically hit her.

"So he got locked up... because of you."

Jah said nothing.

Because yes.

Yes, he did.

Geneva sat on the edge of the dresser, her arms shaking now. "Oh my God, Jahlil."

He rubbed a hand down his face. "I thought I could fix it before it got out of control. I kept thinking, one more win, one more flip, and I'd be good."

She let out a hollow laugh. "And now?"

"I'm drowning."

"You let your brother go to jail. You let this whole family live like we're safe when you've been playing with fire for a year."

Jah didn't respond. Because there wasn't a defense. Only guilt. Shame.

And silence.

Geneva's voice broke again. "Do you even know how dangerous this is?"

He nodded slowly.

"And you didn't think to tell me? Not even once?"

"I didn't want to drag you into it."

She stared at him, voice suddenly quiet. "Jah, I'm already in it. We all are."

Tears welled in her eyes, but they didn't fall. Geneva didn't cry often. And when she did, it meant the damage was permanent.

"I've stood by you through everything," she whispered. "Held this house down. Raised our babies. Prayed over you every night."

Jah's voice was barely audible. "I know."

"No," she snapped. "You don't. Because if you did, you wouldn't have lied to me. You wouldn't have let me think we were good while the floor was caving in under us."

Jah dropped his head.

"I'm sorry."

Geneva looked at him, something cold settling behind her eyes.

"You're not sorry. You're sorry you got caught."

She stood, backing away like she couldn't stand to be near him.

And Jah just sat there.

Watching the space grow between them.

◆ ◆ ◆

A.O.'s office was dim, lit only by the warm glow of a desk lamp and the flicker of city lights pouring in through the window. It was late, past midnight, but neither man had moved in over an hour.

Jah sat across from his brother, elbows on his knees, eyes locked on the floor like it held the words he still hadn't found the courage to say.

A.O. didn't speak.

Didn't rush him.

Just sat back in his chair, quiet, but watching.

Waiting.

Jah finally exhaled, the sound ragged. "I gotta tell you some shit I shoulda said a long time ago."

A.O. leaned back, resting his arms on the chair. "Then say it."

Jah's hands flexed in his lap. His voice was hoarse when he finally began.

"I been gambling."

Still no reaction.

"For years now. On and off. Started small, poker, sports betting. I thought I could control it. I always thought I could stop."

A.O.'s jaw shifted, but he said nothing.

Jah's gaze lifted, barely. "I owe money. Over a hundred thousand. Real street niggas. Not banks."

Silence.

"And the fucked up part is…" He looked away again, shame pressing down on him. "I covered it with money that wasn't mine."

Now A.O. blinked.

Once.

"What money?"

Jah hesitated. His throat worked before the next words came out.

"The bribe. The one you gave me to get the Feds off your back."

A.O. sat still, but his entire presence changed. It was in the way his fingers stopped moving, the way his shoulders pulled back like a weapon about to be drawn.

Jay pushed forward. "I didn't spend all of it. Just enough to buy time. I was planning to flip it back, cover what I took, and make the drop like nothing happened."

A.O. leaned forward slowly.

"But you didn't."

Jah shook his head once. "No."

A.O.'s stare was heavy. Not angry, not yet, but dark. Focused.

"And that's why I got locked up."

Jah swallowed hard. "Yeah."

The silence between them stretched until it became unbearable. The air was thick with disappointment, betrayal, and something colder, something like heartbreak.

"Why the fuck didn't you come to me?" A.O.'s voice was low. Too calm.

Jah's voice cracked. "I didn't want to."

A.O.'s brow lifted slightly. "You didn't want to?"

Jah looked him dead in the eye, and for the first time all night, there was no ducking, no flinching.

"I didn't want you to know I was failing."

A.O. stared at him.

Hard.

Then, after a beat, he leaned back, letting the weight of that sink in.

"You my brother," he said. "My blood. And you thought pride was more important than my freedom?"

Jah's jaw locked. "It wasn't pride. It was shame."

Same difference.

A.O. didn't say it out loud, but the silence spoke for him.

"You always been the smart one," he said finally. "College degree. Big money job. Suits and stock options." He gave a short laugh, but there was no humor in it. "And now you sitting here talking about loan sharks and stolen money."

Jah didn't speak.

Couldn't.

A.O. picked up a glass from the side table and stared into the amber liquid.

"I brought you into this because I trusted you. Thought if anybody could help me run this shit like a business, it was you."

"Then I dragged you into it."

A.O. leaned back again, eyes closed for a moment like he was doing math in his head, counting the weight of every decision that brought them here.

"You know what this did to the crew?" he asked, voice still calm. "You know how many niggas had to move different when I got snatched? How much heat came down just because I was gone?"

Jah nodded.

"Yeah."

A.O. studied him. "And now you want to fix it?"

Jah straightened. "I don't just want to fix it. I will."

A.O. tilted his head slightly. "How?"

The house had cleared out.

But Omar and Jah were still standing in the same room.

Just staring at each other.

Because a decision had to be made.

A.O. had handed them a mission.
Colombia.
Sixty keys.

And Omar?

Omar was ready.

Jah wasn't so sure.

Omar crossed his arms, jaw tight. "So, what's the problem?"

Jah scoffed. "You serious?"

"Dead serious."

Jah dragged a hand over his face. "You think 'cause you dropped some money, you up now? You think you ready for this?"

"I saved your brother," Omar said, voice steady. "I saved all y'all."

Jah didn't blink. "Yeah? And how long before you fuck up again?"

Omar's pulse pounded.

He was tired of the questions.
Tired of the doubt.
Tired of carrying the weight of who he used to be.

"You still see me as the fuck-up, huh?"

Jah's face stayed stone. "I see you for what you are."

Omar's voice dropped. "And what's that?"

"A nigga that never did real work in the streets. A nigga that don't know what it means to carry weight."

The words sliced deep.
But Omar didn't flinch.

He just nodded once, slow and cold.

"Then let's find out."

Jah wasn't just pissed.
He was scared.
Because this wasn't a back alley move. This was cartel business.
And if Omar fucked this up?

They wouldn't just lose money.
They'd lose heads.

Jah sat across from A.O. in the office, the air thick with unspoken heat.

"This ain't the move," Jah said, his voice low but tense.

A.O. leaned back, glass in hand, watching him.

"You think you got a choice?"

Jah clenched his jaw. "This nigga ain't built for this
—"

"And you are?" A.O.'s voice cut through the room like
a blade.

Jah opened his mouth then shut it.

Because that silence?
That was his answer.

A.O. set his glass down, leaned forward.

"Let me tell you something."

Jah braced himself.

"You talk like a nigga who done moved weight. But
you ain't. You was never in this for the life, you just
needed the money."

Jah looked away, the truth landing like bricks on his
chest.

"You had problems before I even called," A.O. said.
"Gambling. Loans. That little hedge fund of yours

was bleeding out before you ever sat at this table."

Jah's throat tightened.

A.O. didn't stop.

"I brought you in 'cause I thought you was smart. Thought you could handle the numbers. But now I'm starting to wonder if you was just another broke nigga pretending to be rich."

Jah stared at the floor.
At the weight of his failures.
At the sound of Geneva's voice in his head, asking about the credit card balances.
Asking why the kids' tuition was late.
Why the mortgage bounced once last month.

And then there was Omar.

Omar, who everybody used to laugh at.
Omar, who they kept in the dark.
Omar, who just risked everything to save them.

"You don't get to sit this one out," A.O. said, voice calm now. Controlled. Final.
"You wanna make moves like a boss? Prove it."

Jah glanced away again.

He thought about the house.

About his daughter's face.

About what it would mean to go home and explain failure to a family that already thought he was winning.

He clenched his jaw.

Nodded once.

"Aight."

18

Omar sat in A.O.'s office, gripping the edge of the desk. His pulse hammered in his ears, but his face was blank.

He had to say it.

Had to get it out before they left.

Jaylen stood off to the side, scrolling through his phone, half paying attention.

A.O. was sitting across from him, sipping his drink, waiting.

Omar exhaled sharply, rubbing the back of his neck.

Then, he said it.

"Sienna's pregnant."

Silence.

Jaylen's head snapped up.

A.O. didn't blink. Didn't react.

He just took another slow sip, then set his glass down.

Finally, he spoke.

"Nigga, you serious?"

Omar nodded once. "Yeah."

Jaylen scoffed, laughing under his breath.

"Nigga, you are the dumbest motherfucker alive."

Omar shot him a glare. "Ain't nobody talking to you."

Jaylen held up a hand. "Nah, you right. I got nothing to say. 'Cause nothing I say gonna change the fact that you fucked your whole life up. Again."

Omar's jaw tightened. "I ain't ask for your opinion."

Jaylen smirked. "And yet, here you are. In a room with niggas that actually handle shit, asking for guidance like a lost puppy."

Omar lunged.

A.O. shot up instantly, stepping between them.

"Enough."

The weight of his voice snapped them both back to reality.

A.O. turned to Omar, his face blank.

"You told Nya?"

Omar exhaled. "No."

A.O. nodded slowly, then leaned back against his desk, rubbing his chin.

"You really got the worst timing, little cousin."

Omar's chest burned. "I ain't plan for this shit, A.O."

A.O. gave him a long look. "But it's happening."

Silence.

Then. A.O. leaned forward, his voice lower.

"So what you wanna do?"

Omar swallowed hard. "Handle my business. Go to Colombia. Prove myself."

A.O. studied him.

"Aight. But if your head ain't in this, don't get on that plane."

Jaylen chuckled, shaking his head. "Nigga already distracted. That baby got your mind spinning. You really think you ready for this trip?"

Omar clenched his fists. "I ain't got a choice."

A.O. smirked slightly, nodding once.

"That's the right answer."

But his eyes?

His eyes said he was watching.

Waiting to see if Omar was gonna fold under pressure.

◆ ◆ ◆

A bottle of liquor rested between them, but neither of them had taken more than a sip.

This wasn't a night to get sloppy.

This was a night to be real.

For once.

Jaylen leaned back in his chair, his gaze fixed on the horizon, the Vegas skyline glowing in the distance.

Omar sat forward, elbows on his knees, rubbing his hands together.

The weight of the trip.
The weight of the baby.
The weight of everything.

It sat heavy on his chest.

Jaylen finally broke the silence, his voice calmer than usual.

"So what you gon' do about this baby situation?"

Omar exhaled slowly, shaking his head. "What the fuck can I do? She keeping it."

Jaylen smirked, shaking his head. "Damn. Nigga, you really fucked up."

Omar scoffed. "Thanks for the insight, Jay. That's real helpful."

Jaylen chuckled, taking a sip from his glass before setting it down.

Then, his expression shifted.

The teasing faded just a little.

"Nah, but for real. You gotta own this shit."

Omar's jaw flexed, but he didn't respond.

Jaylen tapped his fingers against the arm of the chair.

"Look, I ain't gon' act like I got the answers. I ain't a father, I don't got kids, and I don't deal with no baby mama drama. But if you let this situation make you sloppy? It'll ruin you before the baby even gets here."

Omar swallowed hard, his grip tightening on his glass.

Jaylen continued, his voice steady.

"You gotta figure out what kind of man you wanna be. 'Cause right now, all you got is a baby on the way, a crazy ass baby mama, and a trip to Colombia that could go left real fast. You can't afford to be moving emotional, my nigga."

Omar rubbed his forehead. "I ain't moving emotional."

Jaylen side-eyed him. "Yeah? Then why the fuck you just spent the last thirty minutes looking like you tryna solve world peace in your head?"

Omar sighed heavily, shaking his head.

Jaylen smirked, then leaned forward, resting his elbows on his knees.

His voice dropped slightly.

"Listen. I talk a lot of shit about you. And most of the time, you deserve it."

Omar shot him a glare. "Wow, thanks."

Jaylen chuckled, then grew serious again.

"But I can't front. You stepped up when it counted. You bailed us out when we had no options. That was some real nigga shit."

Omar didn't know what to say.

Because Jaylen?

Jaylen never complimented him.

Ever.

Jaylen smirked. "Now, don't get it twisted. That was the dumbest fucking deal I ever seen. But hey, you made the move."

Omar let out a dry chuckle, shaking his head.

Then, after a moment, he half-smirked.

"So... that offer to get rid of Sienna still stand?"

Jaylen let out a full laugh, shaking his head.

"Nigga, I ain't popping a pregnant bitch while I'm out on bond and on trial for a federal RICO case. What kinda idiot you take me for?"

Omar chuckled, shaking his head. "I had to ask."

Jaylen smirked, then grew serious again.

"For real, though. Handle your business. Don't let her play you. And don't let this shit make you slip out there. We got enough problems."

Omar exhaled, nodding slowly.

"I got it."

Jaylen studied him for a second, then nodded once.

"Good. 'Cause I can't save you ass in Columbia from here."

Omar smirked, but his mind was still racing.

Because no matter how much he tried to play it cool...

This trip just got a whole lot more complicated.

19

The morning air was cool, quiet.

The kind of stillness that should have felt peaceful.

But Omar felt anything but peace.

His mind was too loud.

His chest was too tight.

Because today, before he left for Colombia, before he took the biggest risk of his life, he had to face the only thing that ever truly mattered.

His daughter.

When he pulled up to Nya's house, he sat in the car for a long time, gripping the steering wheel, trying to get his thoughts in order.

He had meant to text her first, but he didn't.

Didn't want to give her the chance to tell him no.

Didn't want to give himself an excuse to drive away.

So he took a breath, pushed the car door open, and walked up the familiar path to the front door.

It was different now.

He didn't belong here anymore.

Didn't know if he ever would again.

Before he could talk himself out of it, he knocked.

There was a pause, then the sound of soft footsteps.

The door cracked open just slightly, and for a moment, Nya just looked at him.

Her face was unreadable, her grip on the door firm.

"What are you doing here?" Her voice was calm, but he could hear the exhaustion in it.

Omar swallowed, forcing himself to keep his tone steady. "I wanna see Alya. Before I leave."

Nya exhaled through her nose, looking at him for another long second before stepping back, opening the door wider.

She didn't say anything else, just turned and walked inside.

That was as close to an invitation as he was going to get.

He stepped inside, closing the door behind him, and the moment his eyes landed on Alya, his chest tightened.

She was sitting in the middle of the living room, surrounded by stuffed animals, babbling to herself.

The second she saw him, her whole face lit up.

"Dada!"

The word hit him like a bullet.

Omar exhaled slowly, forcing himself to breathe through the weight of it as he crouched down, opening his arms.

Alya didn't hesitate, she got up, stumbling toward

him on unsteady legs, laughing the whole way.

When she crashed into him, her tiny arms wrapping around his neck, he closed his eyes for a moment, letting himself feel it.

The warmth.
The love.
The innocence.

This was his.

She was his.

But for how much longer?

He held onto her a little tighter, pressing a kiss against her curly little head.

"I missed you, mamas."

Alya just giggled, patting his face with her small hands, completely oblivious to the war inside him.

Completely unaware that her father was about to walk into something that could kill him.

Completely innocent to the fact that he had already fucked up so bad, he might not ever fix it.

He glanced up, his eyes meeting Nya's.

She was leaning against the doorway, arms crossed, watching him carefully.

He couldn't read her.

Didn't know what she was thinking.

Didn't know if she even cared that he was leaving.

But he cared.

And he wanted to say something.

Wanted to talk about them.

Wanted to talk about making things right.

Wanted to tell her that he still saw a future with her, with Alya, with the family he had already lost once.

But he also knew the truth.

If she found out about Sienna's baby, there wouldn't be any future at all.

She would never take him back.

Never forgive him.

And maybe she shouldn't.

Maybe he didn't deserve a second chance.

Maybe this was his karma.

Maybe he would spend the rest of his life trying and failing to put his family back together.

He let out a slow breath, adjusting Alya in his arms.

"I gotta go outta town for a little bit." His voice was quieter than he meant it to be.

Nya raised an eyebrow. "Out of town? Where?"

He hesitated for half a second.

Then he shook his head. "Just business. I'll be back soon."

She studied him for a long moment before nodding slightly. "Mm."

That was all she said.

No more questions.
No more pushing.

Because she knew better than anyone.

If he wasn't telling her, it was because she wouldn't like the answer.

Omar shifted, adjusting Alya again before standing up.

He knew he had to go.

Knew he shouldn't drag this out.

He let himself look at Nya one more time.

That he would never get another moment like this again.

"Nya—"

She shook her head, cutting him off. "Don't."

His throat tightened.

She reached for Alya, and he let her go, his arms suddenly feeling empty.

Like the weight of everything was still there, but without the warmth.

Without the love.

Without her.

He took a step back, nodding slightly. "Aight."

And then he left.

Because there was nothing else to say.

Not yet.

Not when the truth was still waiting to destroy everything

Omar sat in his car outside the airport, his phone in his hand, his stomach tight.

Jah was already inside, probably posted up near the gate, waiting impatiently for him to stop bullshitting.

Their flight left in less than an hour.

But Omar's mind wasn't in Colombia.

It was back home.

Back at Nya's house.

Back where he had just held his daughter, kissed her forehead, let her tiny fingers curl around his, and wondered if he would ever get that moment again.

Because if she found out the truth?

If she found out he had another baby on the way?

He would lose everything.

His hands tightened around the phone.

For a second, he almost convinced himself not to call.

Almost told himself that she wouldn't answer anyway.

But the weight in his chest wouldn't let him leave without trying.

So he exhaled, pressed call, and waited.
The phone rang.

Once.

Twice.

Three times.

He swallowed hard, tapping his fingers against the steering wheel.

"Come on, ma," he muttered under his breath.

Voicemail.

The line cut off.

Her voice came through the speaker, calm, unbothered, so distant it hurt.

"This is Nya. Leave a message."

Beep.

Omar clenched his jaw, closing his eyes.

His breathing was slow, controlled, but his pulse was racing.

He could have hung up.

Could have let it go.

But the words were already there, sitting at the back of his throat, fighting their way out.

So he spoke.

"Hey… it's me."

A stupid start. She knew it was him.

He exhaled sharply, shaking his head, trying again.

"I just—" He hesitated, running a hand over his face. "I'm about to leave for a couple days. Business."

He swallowed hard, gripping the phone tighter.

"I just wanted to hear your voice."

Silence.

"And tell you I love you."

He closed his eyes.

"I know that don't fix shit. I know I fucked up."

His voice dropped lower, rougher.

"But I'm gon' fix it. I swear to God."

He exhaled slowly, leaning back in his seat.

"Just... be safe. And kiss Alya for me."

Silence again.

Then he pressed end.

The second the call cut off, his chest felt heavier.

Because he knew the truth.

She wasn't going to call back.

And when he came home?

She might not even be waiting.

Omar clenched his jaw, shoved his phone in his pocket, and stepped out of the car.

Because dwelling on it wouldn't change a damn thing.

Now?

Now it was time to get on that plane.

And pray that he made it back.

Jah sat still, staring at the seat in front of him, his fingers laced together.

For the first time in a long time, he wasn't stressing about money.

No debt.
No overdue bills.
No loan sharks calling in the middle of the night, threatening to make his family disappear.

He had fixed it.

He had replaced the money he stole.
He had paid off the bribes.
He had cleared the gambling debts.

For now.

But the problem was never just the money.

It was him.

Because no matter how many times he got his finances right, he always found a way to fuck it up again.

Every time he pulled himself out of a hole, he dug another one somewhere else.

And that?

That had to stop.

This time, he had to break the cycle.

Not just for himself, for them.

For Geneva.

For the kids.

For his brother.

Because A.O. was still facing life.

And when A.O. needed him the most, he had failed him.

He had been too proud to ask for help.

Too stubborn to admit how bad things had gotten.

And because of that?

Because of his own ego, his own bullshit?

A.O. sat in a jail cell.

Jah swallowed hard, exhaling slowly, trying to settle
the weight in his chest.

This trip?

This was his chance to fix it.

This wasn't about the money.

This was about redeeming himself.

This was about proving that when A.O. needed him,
he could step up.

That when his wife and kids needed him, he would
be there.

That he wasn't just some washed-up hedge fund

nigga playing gangster.

This time?

He had to be smarter.

No more gambling.
No more lies.
No more digging holes he couldn't climb out of.

He had come too damn close to losing it all.

Now?

Now, he had to make sure he made it home.

For Geneva.
For the kids.
For himself.

Jah sat back, exhaled slowly, and finally closed his eyes.

The intercom buzzed, a voice rolling over the speakers in Spanish first, then English.

"Welcome to Bogotá, Colombia. Local time is 6:37 PM. Please remain seated until the aircraft has come to a complete stop."

There was no turning back now.

20

The house was quiet.

Not just because everyone was gone—but because the decisions had been made. The kind of silence that follows the storm, where everything feels too still. Like the air was holding its breath, waiting to see what came next.

A.O. stood in the hallway just outside his office, one hand resting against the doorframe. The leather of his watch creaked as he flexed his wrist, his fingers tapping absently against the wood. The house had cleared out hours ago. Jah and Omar were gone. Calia and the baby were upstairs. Jaylen and Brandon off somewhere plotting the long route back.

And him?

He was alone.

Still.

Always.

He moved through the house slow, the way someone does when their mind's not fully inside their body. His footsteps didn't echo, but he noticed how heavy they felt. How the sound of them bounced off the walls like the house had grown emptier since he'd been locked up.

It hadn't.

But he had.

He stepped into the living room and sat down, finally letting his body rest. A low exhale slipped out. Not a sigh, just… release.

The glass table in front of him held nothing but a folded sheet of paper and a burner phone. One call could change everything. But that was the problem, wasn't it?

Everything was a gamble now.

He picked up the burner and unlocked it. No missed calls. Just one recording from earlier. He played it again.

Jah's voice. Heated. Defensive.

Omar's voice. Steady, maybe too steady.

And his own voice, calm, cold, final.

"You wanna be in this life? You wanna move like a boss? Then prove it."

He cut the recording off. Tossed the phone back down.

He knew the weight of those words. Knew exactly what he was asking them to carry. But there was no other way. You couldn't build an empire on handouts. You couldn't protect your people by playing it safe.

He leaned forward, elbows on his knees, pressing his hands together, the way he did when he was thinking hard. The liquor sat untouched beside him.

His fingers tapped once.

Twice.

His eyes lifted toward the stairs.

He could hear the faint hum of Malia's baby monitor upstairs. Just white noise. But even that was comforting. Reminded him what all this was for.

His daughter.

His wife.

His legacy.

But none of it would mean shit if this move failed.

He looked down at his hands.

Not shaking.

Not yet.

But that didn't mean the fear wasn't there.

He'd buried more brothers than he could name now. Watched men fold under pressure that was lighter than what he just dropped on Omar and Jah.

Jaylen... solid. But reckless.

Brandon... loyal. But cold inside.

Jah... smart. But breaking.

Omar... heart, but no spine. Not yet.

He'd seen the best of them come and go. And the ones who were still standing? He didn't trust them. Not fully.

Not anymore.

He dragged a hand down his face, rubbing the tension from his jaw.

Then reached for the folded paper on the table.

It was nothing special.

Just notes.

Doodles.

Random shit he'd scribbled during the meeting. But now, looking at it, it felt like a map. Each name. Each arrow. Each underline. He stared at the word he'd written twice.

"Survival."

That was it, wasn't it?

The whole game.

You could call it loyalty. You could call it family. But in the end, it was about survival.

His voice cracked low in his throat before he even realized he was speaking.

"I don't trust nobody. Not really."

His eyes drifted back toward the stairs.

"And the ones I do?" He shook his head. "I just pray they never fold."

His voice was hoarse, like the words had been sitting there for weeks waiting to get out.

He stood again, slower this time.

Grabbed the glass and took a sip.

Didn't wince.

Didn't speak again.

Just stared out the window, where the streetlights cast long shadows across the pavement. Where the world outside kept moving like it didn't know what was about to come crashing down.

And for the first time in a long time?

A.O. wondered if he was moving fast enough to outrun the storm.

◆ ◆ ◆

The casino lights glittered like sin, bouncing off the walls and the glossed-up faces of out-of-towners thinking luck was love in disguise.

But in the backroom?

It was dark.

Quieter than usual.

The soundproofing drowned out the noise from the slots and dice and drunk-ass laughter. Just the low hum of a mini fridge and the flicker of a security screen cycling through camera angles.

Jaylen sat on the edge of the couch, leg bouncing, phone in his hand but face tight with thought. Brandon stood near the door, arms crossed, eyes narrowed at the corner cam feed.

"You feel that?" Jaylen finally said.

Brandon didn't answer right away. Just shifted his weight slightly.

"The silence," Jaylen clarified. "Too fuckin' quiet out there."

Brandon nodded once. "Yeah. I feel it."

They both knew what that kind of quiet meant.

Not peace.

Pressure.

Corners that used to buzz all day now had gaps in the line. Runners missing shifts. Product moving slow. Folks whispering more than they were buying.

Jaylen leaned back, chewing on the inside of his cheek. "It don't feel right, B. Not since we got out. Shit was moving fine when we was locked."

Brandon cut his eyes over. "Deonte."

Jaylen smirked bitter. "Nigga couldn't wait, huh?"

Brandon shook his head. "He took his shot. Don't mean he hit."

Jaylen snorted. "He ain't miss either."

A long pause stretched between them. Jaylen's jaw clenched like he was holding something back. Like violence was his second language and he was trying real hard to speak English.

Then he stood, pacing a little.

"Niggas out here actin' like we just gone stay quiet. Like A.O. came home and forgot how to move."

Brandon didn't look up. Just said, calm and even, "A.O. told us to chill."

Jaylen turned. "And that ain't got your skin itching?"

Brandon gave a half-shrug. "Course it do. But we follow order. We ain't no crash dummies."

Jaylen paced again. "You ain't see how them lil' niggas was actin' on Cedar yesterday? Muggsy wouldn't even make eye contact. Niggas nervous. Spooked."

Brandon finally met his eyes. "That's cause they know shit shifting. They don't know where the lines are yet."

Jaylen's face darkened. "They gon' learn. One way or another."

His phone buzzed in his hand.

He glanced down, about to ignore it, but froze.

Brandon noticed. "Who that?"

Jaylen answered, but didn't move away.

"Yo."

A soft voice came through the speaker. "Uncle Jay?"

He blinked. "Chasiti?"

"Daddy's phone not working. He said he'd call me after practice but he didn't. Is he okay?"

Jaylen glanced toward Brandon, then walked into the corner of the room for some privacy.

"Yeah, baby. He good. Just busy right now. You alright?"

A small sniffle. "Yeah. Just wanted to say I got a solo next week. For the play."

Jaylen smiled, just a little. "That's big, C. I'm proud of you."

She giggled shyly. "You gonna come?"

He hesitated. "You know I will."

"You always say that."

Jaylen's jaw tightened. "I mean it this time. I swear."

"Okay," she whispered. "Tell Daddy I said call me."

"I will, baby. Love you."

"Love you too."

He hung up, staring at the black screen like it owed him something.

Brandon was watching. Quiet. "You good?"

Jaylen sat back down, wiping a hand over his face. "I ain't built for this double life shit, man."

Brandon shrugged. "We all livin' two lives. Some of us just better at it."

Jaylen looked at him. "You ever get tired?"

Brandon didn't answer right away.

But his phone buzzed too. A text.

From his sister.

"Can you grab diapers? Got off late."

He slid the phone back in his pocket without replying.

Then looked at Jaylen and said, "Every fuckin' day."

Another beat of silence passed before Brandon spoke again.

"But we still here."

Jaylen leaned forward, elbows on his knees. "I'm ready to go to war. Like... now."

Brandon shook his head. "That's the problem. You always ready to move, but never ready to wait."

Jaylen scowled. "Waitin' got us hemmed up last time."

"Runnin' in blind gone get us killed."

Jaylen didn't argue.

Didn't agree either.

Brandon pushed off the wall and walked over, standing above him.

"Look, I want this nigga gone too. Deonte ain't never been solid. But A.O. got a plan. And if we move before he say move?"

Jaylen looked up.

Brandon's voice dropped.

"Then we ain't soldiers. We liabilities."

Jaylen stared at him, then let out a long breath.

"Aight."

Brandon nodded once.

Then, softer, more to himself than anyone else, he muttered, "We get one shot to do this right. One."

Jaylen stood again, tension still riding his frame.

"But when the greenlight come?"

Brandon's eyes narrowed.

"I'm already loaded."

Deonte wasn't in his usual spot tonight.
He hated this side of town.
Too many cameras. Too many fake tough niggas.
But the intel?
The intel was worth it.

He leaned against the back wall of a dark, nearly empty smoke lounge, hood-rich ambiance, velvet couches, low lights, music low enough to hear a man think.

Across from him sat a skinny, jittery dude in a work hoodie with a casino logo stitched crooked on the chest.

"You got two minutes," Deonte said flatly.

The worker licked his lips. "Aight, so last night... I was changin' the bulbs in the back hallway. Right behind that little side room Jaylen and Brandon be meetin' in—"

"You was eavesdroppin'?" Deonte cut in, one brow raised.

"Nah, nah... I mean, the door was cracked. I wasn't even tryna hear nothin', but—"
He leaned in. "They talkin' about Colombia."

Deonte didn't react. Just sipped his drink.

"They movin' weight. Big weight. Said it's comin' straight from the source. Sixty bricks. Omar flyin' in with A.O. and some chick. Jaylen and Brandon drivin' back with they half."

That made Deonte look up.

"Jaylen... movin' bricks?"
He chuckled under his breath. "Since when?"

The worker shrugged. "Ion know. But they was stressin'. Said they gotta move quiet 'cause the feds still circlin'. Said this move gon' put 'em back on top."

Deonte nodded slowly.

Back on top.

That's what this was about.

"They said how soon?" he asked.

"Few days. Jaylen said they already got a front setup —some beauty brand or sum'n. Hella boxes. All sealed and wrapped. Said they movin' like customs can't touch 'em."

The drink hit the back of Deonte's throat, warm and smooth.

"Who else know?"

The worker hesitated. "Just me. I ain't told nobody. Look—I ain't no snitch, I'm just tryna—"

Deonte waved him off. "Relax."

He stood slowly, walked to the window, staring out at the lot.

The streets were too quiet lately.
But now he knew why.

A.O. was gearing up for war.

Trying to rise from the ashes.

Bringing in that international dope like he still had soldiers everywhere.

Like the game hadn't changed.

But this time?

This time Deonte had the head start.

He turned back around.

"You did good," he said. "Real good."

The worker looked surprised. "So we straight?"

Deonte nodded, pulled a folded stack from his coat, tossed it on the table.

"We straight."

The worker reached for the cash fast—too fast—and started to stand.

But Deonte held up one finger.

"One more thing," he said, voice low. "You ain't never hear nothin' else. And you damn sure don't repeat this to nobody."

The worker paused, halfway up. "Nah, of course not."

Deonte gave him a look.

The kind that let a man know he was one mistake from vanishing.

"Cool."

He watched the worker leave, then picked up his phone.

One text.
To one person.

Move the stash.
We got company comin'.

Then he sat back down, alone in the smoke, smiling to himself for the first time in weeks.

A.O. thought he was rebuilding.

Deonte?

He was already cracking the foundation.

Part Two Coming Soon

In The Black Enterprise: Blood Brothers, enemies close in from every side—Deonte's making moves, and not everyone in the crew is built to withstand the pressure. Loyalty gets tested, and money ain't enough to keep everyone quiet.

A.O. is holding it all together by a thread, but even kings get tired.

Jaylen's losing patience. Brandon's seeing ghosts.

And Omar? He's about to learn that running from your past only makes it catch up harder.

In Part Two of The Black Enterprise, bonds will break. Blood will spill.

The truth is coming to everbody.